Please return / renew by date shown.

It took her breath away.

Matt was kissing her, shaping her body with his hands as though he couldn't get enough of her, and she realised that she wanted this, needed it.

She clung to him, kissing him fiercely in return, loving every moment, her body on fire where his hands caressed her.

'You can't imagine how difficult it's been keeping away from you when all I wanted to do was hold you in my arms,' Matt said.

'Why did you hold back?' Lucy whispered softly.

He sighed, bending his head so that his cheek lay against hers. 'All sorts of reasons...and all of them are just as valid now.'

Dear Reader

There's something really special about college days, with young people, so full of energy and sparkle, living life to the full. Everything takes on the brightest colours. Their lives are filled with music, deep, lasting friendships and the sheer joy of being alive and trying new things.

So when the four young people in my book get together to share a house, things are bound to fizz. It isn't long before Jade and Ben find themselves drawn to one another... Things are definitely beginning to warm up but, as always, there are pitfalls along the way. Jade is cautious about getting involved— and anyway, what with all her studies, and working part-time at a café-bar in London, whenever would she find the time for a relationship?

And what of the other two people in the house? Well, Lucy and Matt are certainly a mismatched couple... Jade and Ben are well used to observing their frequent spats. But when they have to work together as well as live together, sooner or later things are bound to change.

I loved finding out how these young people interacted with one another. I hope you do too.

With love

Joanna

DR RIGHT
ALL ALONG

BY
JOANNA NEIL

MILLS
BOON®

First published in Great Britain 2012
by Mills & Boon, an imprint of Harlequin (UK) Limited.
Large Print edition 2012
Harlequin (UK) Limited, Eton House,
18-24 Paradise Road, Richmond, Surrey TW9 1SR

© Joanna Neil 2012

ISBN: 978 0 263 22478 8

Harlequin (UK) policy is to use papers that are natural, renewable and recyclable products and made from wood grown in sustainable forests. The logging and manufacturing process conform to the legal environmental regulations of the country of origin.

Printed and bound in Great Britain
by CPI Antony Rowe, Chippenham, Wiltshire

When **Joanna Neil** discovered Mills & Boon®, her lifelong addiction to reading crystallised into an exciting new career writing Mills & Boon® Medical Romance™. Her characters are probably the outcome of her varied lifestyle, which includes working as a clerk, typist, nurse and infant teacher. She enjoys dressmaking and cooking at her Leicestershire home. Her family includes a husband, son and daughter, an exuberant yellow Labrador and two slightly crazed cockatiels. She currently works with a team of tutors at her local education centre, to provide creative writing workshops for people interested in exploring their own writing ambitions.

CHAPTER ONE

'YOU'RE cutting it a bit fine, aren't you?' Matt Berenger frowned as Lucy hurried into the kitchen. 'Aren't you supposed to be starting your new placement at the hospital at eight o'clock this morning? That gives you less than half an hour.'

'Tell me about it!' Lucy groaned. She dumped her holdall down on a chair and ran her fingers through her silky golden hair, as though the action would in some way help to clear her head. 'I left my parents' home at six this morning, thinking I'd have plenty of time, but there was an accident on the road, and before I knew it I was in a tailback half a mile long. I hope whoever was involved will be all right. I passed a couple of ambulances, but I couldn't see what was going on.'

She opened a cupboard door and peered inside. 'I'm starving. I didn't have any breakfast before

I left because I thought I'd be able to last until I arrived back here.' She frowned. The cupboard was practically empty.

'You forgot to get the groceries in before you went away for the weekend,' Matt remarked in a dry tone. He walked over to the coffeemaker and flicked a switch.

Lucy stared at him distractedly for a moment or two. He was wearing dark trousers and a freshly laundered linen shirt, and he looked fit and ready for anything—a huge contrast to her sleep-deprived, travel-weary self. Long limbed, lean and muscular, his presence seemed to dominate the small kitchen. It was a little unnerving. She hadn't even expected to find him here this morning. She'd been sure he would have set off for the hospital well before she'd arrived home.

'We're out of everything,' he added, 'barring milk.'

She winced, coming back to earth with a bit of a jolt. 'Oh, heavens, I'm sorry…it was my turn to get the food in, wasn't it? I'll have to get a grip. I meant to do it, I know I did, but something must have come up.' She shook her head in frustration, causing her long tresses to sway and then settle in a shimmering cloud over her shoulders as she tried to remember what it was that had caused her to forget. 'It was Jade, I think…she told me she and Ben had bought a house, and she wanted me to go and see it with her. I was going to do the shopping on the way back, before I left for Berkshire, but…'

'But then I guess something else cropped up.' Matt poured coffee into a mug and handed it to her. 'Here, drink this. Perhaps it'll help you get your head together.' He studied her for a moment or two, his penetrating blue glance moving over the smooth lines of the dress that draped itself lovingly around her curvaceous figure. He blinked, falling silent for a while before giving himself a shake and bringing his mind back to the situation at hand. 'I thought you planned on coming back last night?'

She nodded. 'I did, but Mum and Dad invited family friends round at the last minute, and it would have been rude to leave since I'd not seen them in a while.' Hunger pangs clawed at her stomach and she stared in dismay at the cupboard once more. There was a fog clouding her brain and she couldn't think what to do.

'There's half a slice of toast left over from my breakfast,' he said. 'You might want to eat that. I was going to put it out for the birds, but I'm sure your need is greater than theirs.' He gave a wry smile and pushed a plate towards her. 'I'd have done the shopping myself but I was on call over the weekend. I didn't get home until late last night.'

She sent him a quick look. 'Thanks for this,' she murmured, spreading butter on the cold toast and munching gratefully.

'You're welcome. It's a bit pale around the edge because the bread slices are too big for the toaster—I had to hunt it out because the grill on the cooker isn't working.'

'It tastes perfect to me.' She frowned. 'I'll have to get someone in to look at the cooker.' She bit into the toast once more, and after a while she said, 'You must be shattered. Do you have to go in to work again today?' From the way he was dressed, she guessed he wasn't going to be lounging around the house.

'I do. It's not too bad, though. I'm part of a good team—I'm being given the chance to do procedures we only practised in med school, and being on call means I get to take on a lot more responsibility. It's what I want.'

Lucy nodded, finishing off her toast and brushing the crumbs from her fingers. She swallowed the last of her coffee. 'This year's gone well for you, hasn't it? I suppose, with any luck, I'll be in the same position as you, a foundation-year doctor, by August…except that I have to get through my final exams first.' She thought about that and pulled a face. 'I'm really not looking forward to those. I'm spending every last minute revising.' Finding that time was becoming more and more difficult of late, though. Much as she loved her parents, she could have done without going home this particular weekend.

She hunted around for her bag, and said hurriedly, 'I have to go. What time do you have to be on duty?'

He glanced at his watch. 'Soon. I'll walk with you.'

'Okay.'

It was a strange feeling, being alone with Matt like this, and she wasn't sure quite how she felt about it. There were usually four of them sharing the house, but things had changed now that Jade and Ben were planning their wedding. They had been house hunting, and hadn't been around very much of late.

Perhaps that was why Matt had been acting differently these last few weeks. It was an odd situation. He'd been surprisingly laid-back about her forgetting to get the groceries, and that in itself was peculiar, given the way he usually enjoyed teasing her.

'You said Jade took you to see the house they'd bought,' Matt commented now, cutting in on her thoughts. They left the neat, Georgian crescent of houses behind them and set out along the London streets, heading for the hospital. 'I imagine that means they'll be wanting to move out fairly soon.'

She shook her head. 'It'll be some time before they do that, I think. With prices being what they are in London, they've settled for a house that needs quite a bit of work. They have to rewire the place and put in central heating, and so on, and after that they'll be decorating.'

He pulled a face. 'That sounds like a lot of hard work.'

She smiled. 'I don't think they mind. It'll be a great house once the renovations have been done. And I guess, as long as they're together, they'll be happy enough. I suppose it could be fun, getting the place just how they want it.'

He gave her a sidelong glance, lifting a dark brow. 'Fun? Well, yes, it's the sort of thing I'd enjoy. I can see how it would be good to stamp your individual touch on a house, to make it well and truly your own, but I can't imagine you wanting to do hands-on stuff like that. With your background, I'd have thought you'd be more inclined to get the builders in.' The hint of a smile touched his lips as his gaze wandered to her beautifully manicured nails.

'Oh, here we go…' she remarked in a cross voice. 'Why does everyone assume they know me from a quick glance at the way I look? And you're a prime example. We might have lived in the same house for the last few months, but you don't know me at all, do you? You just think that you do. I'm perfectly capable of setting to and fixing things up if need be.'

Not that she'd ever been called on to do anything like that, but it didn't mean she wouldn't be capable if the situation arose, did it?

'Okay, okay…I take it back. There's no need to get yourself worked up about it. I didn't mean to ruffle your feathers.' His mouth quirked and she frowned, looking at him suspiciously. Was she overreacting? It had been a difficult weekend, one way and another, and she had to admit to being tired and out of sorts.

She was silent for a moment or two, thinking things through. It looked as though she and Matt would be on their own in the house for a good deal of the time from now on, and that could be difficult for both of them, without Jade and Ben there to deflect their arguments. They were opposites, after all. Matt was laid-back, easygoing, happy to strum on his guitar whenever the fancy took him, whereas she…

She had a lot to contend with, even more so of late since her father had decided to expand his business. The changes meant there was far more work to be done. Lucy was a medical student, but she'd always helped out with her parents' property development company, ever since she had been old enough to hold the other end of a measuring tape. She'd been round countless properties with her father and grandfather, and knew the jargon off pat—strengthen those joists, put in a new damp course, sand the wooden floors. Even now, her father regularly sent work her way.

'See if you can track down a supplier for those ceramic tiles I want for the old-cottage renovations, will you?' he'd said last week. 'And have a look on the internet to see if there are any likely properties in the neighbouring area. Find out how much the houses go for over there. You can fill me in on the details when you come over at the weekend. Your mother's looking forward to having you with us for Sunday lunch, and I want to show you the old farm cottage now that the work is almost finished.'

All these things took time, when she really ought to be studying, but she didn't complain. After all, her father owned this house that they were all living in, and she, at least, didn't have to pay rent. No doubt Matt thought she was a spoiled daddy's girl, but in reality she paid her way by working as a researcher for her father.

It wasn't fair, the way she was judged. Just because she came from a wealthy family, and she happened to be blonde with a decent figure, people only saw the superficial, the outer packaging. They saw a golden-haired fashion model, and assumed she was only interested in looking good and keeping up with the latest fashion trends.

It was the same at the hospital. She had to work harder than anyone else to be accepted as the woman she really was, someone who would one day make a skilled and capable doctor.

That was what she hoped she would become, anyway. If she didn't get there, it wouldn't be for want of trying.

'You'll be working on Paediatrics for the next week or so, won't you?' Matt asked, sniffing the air as they passed by a café. The proprietors were setting up for the day and the appetising smell of meat pasties and hot bacon wafted through the air.

Lucy's mouth watered, and she thought longingly of food...crisp bacon, eggs with bright yellow yolks, and maybe a couple of hash browns to complete the meal... She groaned inwardly; the toast Matt had given her had only served as an appetiser. She didn't even like fried food, so why on earth was she obsessing about it now?

'Yes, that's right,' she said. 'Jade told me she had a good experience on Professor Farnham's team, so I'm hoping things will turn out pretty much the same for me. I'm not sure how I'll cope, though, working with children.'

'I'm sure you'll be fine.' He laid a hand on the small of her back and urged her through the automatic doors at the entrance to the hospital. 'I must go and meet up with my consultant. Perhaps we'll catch up with one another later on?'

Even though he removed his hand, she still felt its warm imprint on her spine as they walked along the corridor towards the lift bay. It was a peculiar, intimate feeling, and she pulled in a quick breath to help her deal with the strange emotions that had suddenly overtaken her.

'Perhaps.' She nodded in agreement, though with any luck they'd go their separate ways. She still wasn't sure quite how to deal with this new-style Matt. Over the last few months, she'd become used to their frequent, fairly good-natured spats, but now that he was being halfway nice to her she didn't know how to take it.

She went straight to the children's ward and introduced herself to the registrar on duty and to the nursing staff.

'It's good to see you again, Lucy,' the registrar greeted her with a smile. They'd met before and talked occasionally whenever there had been a gig going on in the student union bar, and the last few times he had made a point of singling her out. James Tyler was tall and good-looking, in his mid-thirties, and she was sure he would be a catch for any girl but she wasn't inclined to get involved with him, no matter how much he pushed the issue.

She'd been bitten a couple of times before, and he had all the hallmarks of being like the other men in her life—seduced by the way she looked, and interested only in one thing. She just wasn't prepared to go down that route again, especially not at this particular time when she was completing the most difficult year of her medical studies.

'You, too,' she murmured, and listened attentively as he briefly outlined the case histories of the young patients in the unit.

'Professor Farnham wants you to check on all the youngsters, and make yourself familiar with their conditions, and their treatment, medications and so on. When you've done that, he'd like you to take a look at the baby in here,' he said, taking her over to the neighbouring bay. 'See what you make of him. He's ten months old.'

'Do I get to look at his notes?'

He smiled. 'Later. I think the professor wants to see what you come up with first.'

Lucy drew in a deep breath. 'Okay. I'll do my best.'

'Good. I'll leave you to it, if you don't mind. I have to go and see to a patient who's being admitted. The professor should be along in around an hour's time—he's been liaising with A and E over a ten-year-old who was injured in a traffic accident on the bypass this morning. We'll be looking after him. The boy has a splenic injury, but he may not need surgery if we can keep him on supportive treatment for a while.'

Lucy frowned. 'That must have been the accident I came across when I was on my way home from my parents' house, first thing. Do you know if anyone else was injured?'

'His parents escaped with minor injuries, and the driver of the other car has a broken arm. It seems they were lucky, all things considered. The boy was hurt when the side of the car was pushed inwards.'

'Well, I'm glad I found out what happened to them, anyway.'

He moved away from her and Lucy went to introduce herself to the children on the ward. Some of them were very poorly, whilst others were on the way to recovery and greeted her cheerfully.

When she had finished getting to know them, she went back to the bay where her special patient, the ten-month-old baby, was sleeping. She walked over to the cot and gazed down at the tiny, pale-looking infant. He was receiving oxygen through thin tubes inserted in his nostrils, and when she looked at the monitors, she could see that his blood oxygen level was very low. He was breathing fast, and even with the oxygen therapy it seemed as though he was struggling to get enough air into his lungs.

'You poor little thing,' she murmured. 'I'm going to disturb you for just a minute or two, poppet, while I listen to your chest.' She put the earpieces of the stethoscope into her ears and warmed the chest piece with her hands before running it over the baby's lungs.

'What have you managed to find out, Lucy? Anything interesting?'

She jumped as Professor Farnham suddenly appeared at her side. Even more startling was the fact that Matt was with him. She looked at both of them, wide-eyed, before recovering herself and sliding the stethoscope back around her neck.

'I—uh...' What was Matt doing here? He wasn't meant to be on this team, was he? The professor was waiting for an answer, though, and she hurriedly pulled herself together. 'There are decreased breath sounds bilaterally and I heard inspiratory crackles, suggesting involvement of the deeper lung tissues. He has a high fever, he's breathing fast and has shortness of breath. I'd say he was suffering from a severe chest infection, possibly pneumonia.'

The professor nodded. 'And what procedures would you carry out?'

She gave it some thought. 'Blood cultures, sputum sample and chest X-ray.'

'Good, well done. Keep that up and you'll get through your clinical exams without any trouble at all.' He beamed at her. He was a tall, slim man, in his mid-fifties, she guessed, with dark brown hair that was beginning to grey a little at the sides. His hazel eyes showed an alert, keen intelligence. 'The tests have already been done. Let's see what the lab came up with, shall we?' He moved over to the computer at the other side of the room, leaning over the table and pressing a few keys.

While the professor was otherwise engaged, Lucy sent Matt a narrowed glance. 'What are you doing here?' she mouthed silently.

'New rotation,' he mouthed back. 'Paediatric medicine and intensive care.'

A small surge of dismay flowed through her. He could have told her before this, couldn't he? As things were, it had come as something of a shock to discover that they would be working together, and she felt as though she had been completely wrong-footed. Why had he held back from telling her?

'I thought it might put you off your stride if I told you this morning,' he whispered, as though he had read her mind. 'I only got the placement at the last minute when someone dropped out.'

'Here we are,' Professor Farnham said. 'The test results are on screen. What do you make of them, Lucy?'

Discomfited, she hoped he wouldn't notice the warm colour that had flooded her cheeks. She hated being put on the spot like this, with Matt looking on.

She went over to the table and studied the lab report. 'It's a bacterial infection—*Staphylococcus aureus*.' She brought the X-ray film up on screen and studied it for a while. 'Definitely pneumonia,' she decided, 'though there's something else going on there.' She hesitated, unsure of what she was seeing. 'There appears to be some inflammation in the pleural space.'

'What do you think, Matt?' The professor waved Matt forward so that he could have a look.

'I think she's right. It could be an empyema,' he said, 'a collection of pus in the cavity between the lung and the inside of the chest wall. I expect that's why the baby is in so much distress.'

The consultant nodded. 'Usually, these things clear up with antibiotic treatment, but he's already been given that. We might be dealing with a secondary infection here. I don't think we can leave this one—perhaps you'd like to do the chest-drainage procedure? That should reduce the pressure and help the baby to breathe more comfortably. We'll get the sample analysed and then we can see what kind of antibiotic we need to add to the mix.'

'I'd be glad to do it.' Matt turned to look at the baby, his expression serious. 'I'll set up the equipment right away.'

'Excellent. Lucy can help you with that—in fact, it might be a good idea if she were to shadow you for the next week or so.' He sent Matt a querying look. 'It'll give her a good insight into what goes on in Paediatrics.'

Matt hesitated just for a moment, and then said, 'That's fine. I'm okay with that.'

Lucy held her breath for a second or two, trying to take it in. She was to follow Matt around? Her mind skittered, seeking a way out of the situation, before coming around to the inevitable conclusion that there was no escape.

She had to be professional about this, of course. Obviously the professor had no idea how she and Matt tended to avoid one another back at the house, if only for the sake of peace and quiet. Something that had been easy enough when Jade and Ben had been around, but now…? She was doomed. Not only were they being thrown together at home, now they were to work together, as well. How long would it be before they found themselves at loggerheads over something or other?

Matt looked at her, and for a moment their glances met, each of them keeping their innermost thoughts hidden.

'I'll leave things with you, then,' Professor Farnham said. 'Any problems, and James will be around to help you out.'

Lucy looked anxiously at the baby after the professor had left. 'He's so small and vulnerable,' she said softly. 'I'm glad it's not me having to do an invasive procedure on him. Are you okay with it?' She sent Matt a troubled look. She felt unnaturally queasy at the thought.

He shrugged. 'It has to be done if he's to get better,' he murmured. 'Let's take him over to the treatment room, and then we'll scrub up.'

She went with him and helped him to lay out a trolley with the necessary medical equipment. It was something she'd seen done many times, and she knew well enough how to clean the baby's skin and drape the chest area with dressings.

Matt sedated the baby, and all appeared to be well. Even so, her stomach lurched as he anaesthetised the area and prepared to make the incision. She didn't know what was wrong with her. It was odd, this feeling of being out of synch with everything. She was usually on the ball and quite happy to go along with whatever procedure was needed.

Matt carefully identified the area over the baby's rib and began to insert the chest tube. Lucy felt a wave of nausea swell up inside her.

It threatened to overwhelm her, and immediately she began to panic. All of a sudden she felt hot, with beads of perspiration breaking out on her brow, and her heart was pounding so much that she could feel it in her throat. She felt faint.

This couldn't be happening to her, not here, not now. Whatever would Matt think of her if she were to disgrace herself by being sick, here in the treatment room?

'Are you all right?' he asked, pausing as he checked that the tube was in place.

'I'm fine,' she managed, keeping her head down. She handed him the collecting device and he connected the tube to it so that the drained fluid could be accumulated and made available for testing.

'You don't look all right,' he commented. 'You're very pale. Are you going to be sick?'

She shook her head and swallowed hard. She wouldn't allow herself to be sick. Heavens above, she'd seen this operation performed many times before, and it didn't make sense that now, of all times, she should want to throw up.

'We'll have to take him down to X-Ray to make sure that the tube is in the right place,' he said.

She nodded. 'I'll just… I'll… Excuse me a minute, will you?' The way she was feeling, she knew she wouldn't make it as far as Radiology, so she grabbed the opportunity to escape. Their work was more or less done here, and she wouldn't be missed for a minute or two, would she? All she could think about was getting outside and finding some fresh air before she made a complete fool of herself.

It was probably too late, anyway. Matt had already guessed that she wasn't feeling well, and he would come to the only possible conclusion, that she wasn't fit to be a doctor if she felt faint assisting with a commonplace surgical procedure.

She didn't wait for Matt to answer. Instead, she headed outside and made for the paved area set out in the L-shape created by the wall of the children's ward where it met up with the treatment area. Fortunately for her there was no one around, and she found a bench to sit on, where she bent forward and put her head between her knees.

She stayed like that for a few minutes, only coming up for air when the nausea had passed.

'Are you feeling any better now?' For the second time that day, Matt startled her by arriving when he was least expected.

'Oh,' she said, looking at him aghast. 'I thought… I thought I was on my own out here.'

He nodded. 'It's okay. No one else knows but me. How are you?'

'Better,' she admitted. 'Much better. I'm sorry I rushed out on you. I don't know what came over me. Is the baby okay? Does he still need to go to X-Ray?'

'I asked the nurse to take him over there.' He studied her, his dark eyes brooding. 'I'm guessing you're not likely to be pregnant, so the other explanation for you feeling ill could be lack of food. Let's get you over to the cafeteria, and you can get some proper food inside you.'

She shook her head. 'I can't do that—I have to

get on. Professor Farnham wants to see my case notes. He'll want to know where I am.'

He frowned. 'I doubt he'll be waiting with bated breath. Did you eat properly while you were at your parents' house?'

'Of course I did.' She looked at him, astonished that he could think otherwise. 'Though…well, I missed tea, because I went with Dad to look over one of his projects, and by the time we arrived back at the house there were visitors waiting for us.' She thought things through. 'I should have made myself a snack for supper, I suppose, but it was late and I was so tired I just wanted to crawl into bed.'

He raised a dark brow. 'I thought going home was supposed to be relaxing?'

She gave him a wan smile. 'You know how my father is. He never stops. He's always on the lookout for new properties to develop. And whenever I did get half an hour to myself, I switched on my laptop and did some work for my exams.'

'Lord help us.' He rolled his eyes heavenwards.

'You won't even reach first base as a doctor if you don't know how to keep yourself healthy.'

She mulled that over for a while. Of course, he was right. He must have a very low opinion of her, and she deserved it. It was very depressing, and all at once she was swamped with guilt for letting things get to this state.

'Come on,' Matt said. 'I'll take you along to the cafeteria.' He placed a hand beneath her elbow and helped her to her feet. 'And don't even think of asking for a salad. Jade told me you keep that perfect figure by cutting out pasta and fries, and anything else that might tend to add the pounds. That's a silly way to be going on. You have to be at the top of your game, for heaven's sake. You need nourishment.'

Jade had been talking about her? How could she do that with Matt, of all people?

'I know that,' she protested. 'If I don't eat those foods, it's because I'm not keen on them. It's nothing to do with watching my weight. I don't do that—I don't even think about it.'

He made a disgruntled, scoffing sound and

urged her on, walking with her through the entrance door and along the corridor towards the cafeteria.

'Sit down,' he said, when they arrived there and he had picked out a table by the window. 'I'll go and order for you.'

He started to walk away. 'Hey, hang on a minute,' Lucy called after him. 'You don't even know what I want.' She frowned, feeling unaccountably annoyed. Perhaps that was another side effect arising from lack of sleep and practically nothing to eat.

He turned and looked at her as though he was dealing with a recalcitrant child. 'I thought pancakes with strawberry syrup, and waffles with ice cream on the side. That way you get to eat and be cheered up at the same time. Those are your favourites, aren't they?'

'Well, um, yes…but…' How did he know that? She didn't even know that he must have been watching her over these last few months. Waffles and ice cream for breakfast? She weighed it up in her mind. Then again, why not? 'Oh, what the heck…' She gave up the struggle and saw the faint smile that tugged at the corners of his mouth.

Then he swivelled around, and she watched him stride over to the counter to place the order. He was still shaking his head as though he was trying to fathom how they had come to be in this situation. She hated the fact that she'd had to be rescued by him. It would have been so much simpler if they could have gone on passing each other like ships in the night. That way, neither one of them would have needed to try to understand the other.

When he came back to the table a few minutes later he was carrying a tray that was filled with goodies, along with two steaming cups of coffee. 'That should do the trick,' he murmured, laying the dishes in front of her. 'Tuck in.'

She didn't need a second bidding. Only when she'd finished with the pancakes and was ready to start on the waffles did she look up at him and notice that he was working his way through a burger and chips.

'First rule of medicine,' he said. 'Make sure that you're fuelled up and ready to go.'

'I'll remember that,' she murmured. She smiled, relaxing for the first time that morning, and he stopped eating, looking at her oddly, as though he'd never really seen her before.

'I wasn't expecting to be working with you,' he said, after a while. 'That might take some getting used to for both of us.'

'Yes, I expect so.' She gave him a fleeting glance before turning her attention to the waffles, still warm from the grill, with ice cream slowly melting into the syrupy hollows. 'You said you were given this placement at the last minute. What happened to the one you'd already chosen?'

'I had to talk to the consultants about it. I really wanted to do Paediatrics, and the opportunity seemed too good to miss. I didn't think they'd go for it, but in the end they seemed happy to change things around, and so here I am.'

She nodded, finishing off her dessert and leaning back in her chair, a satisfied expression on her face.

'The colour's come back into your cheeks,' he said. 'That's good.' He looked as though he was about to say something more, but then his phone started to play its familiar tune, a lilting guitar melody, and he sent her an apologetic look. 'I'd better get this.'

He studied the caller ID, and then said, 'Hello, Mum. What's up? It's not like you to call this early in the day.'

He frowned as the conversation developed. 'Chest pains? How long has he been getting them?' There was a moment or two of silence while he listened, and then he said, 'Make sure he goes along to his GP. I'll come over to see you, if you like… No? Well, yes, you're probably right—but let me know how he goes on, won't you?' Another period of quiet followed, before he added, 'Yes, I know, but they're partners, and he was bound to take on the bulk of the work when the business started to expand.'

He cut the call a while later, and Lucy gave him a sympathetic glance. She wasn't sure whether she ought to intrude, but she was sitting here with him, and she hadn't been able to help hearing what had been said.

'Was that about your father?' she asked quietly. 'Is he ill?' There had also been something about 'the business' and that worried her, because Matt's father was in partnership with her father, and it sounded as though there was a problem of some sort.

Matt pressed his lips together, making them into a flat line. 'My mother's worried about him. He's been working too hard lately, and now he's getting twinges in his chest.' His gaze met hers. 'The trouble is, he always puts in a hundred and ten per cent. We've tried telling him to slow down, but he doesn't listen. He says he doesn't have a choice.'

'Because of my father? That's what you're thinking, isn't it?'

His shoulders lifted, but he didn't reply, and his expression was unreadable, leaving her at a loss. Of course he blamed her father. Martyn Clements was a powerhouse of energy, and the business meant everything to him. He drove himself and

everyone else to give their utmost to make it succeed. He'd never come to terms with the fact that
his daughter chose to study medicine rather than
carry on in his footsteps.

'We should get back to the children's unit,' he
said, his features grim and impenetrable.

'Yes.' She hesitated. 'What will you do?'

'Nothing, for the moment,' he answered. 'I'll
go and see him at the weekend.'

She followed him out of the cafeteria and neither of them spoke. A wall had come down between them, and the relaxed atmosphere of just
a few minutes ago had passed. The loss left her
with a hollow feeling inside.

CHAPTER TWO

'IT LOOKS as though you've bought enough food to last us for a month,' Jade observed with a laugh, watching Lucy stocking up the fridge and freezer. 'I can't see how the groceries kitty would have covered us for that lot.'

'No…well, I was worried about leaving the cupboards empty, so I decided to get a few extras in. Nothing major, but a few things to tide us over in an emergency—dried milk, bread for the freezer, pasta shells and sauces, rice and curry spices and chicken pieces. That way we'll always have something to fall back on.'

Jade smiled. 'Ah…now I see the reason for the shopping spree. So Matt's been giving you a hard time, has he?'

'No, no…not at all.' Lucy paused, thinking about that. 'Actually, he's been remarkably quiet, lately. He hardly said a word when we ran out of everything at the weekend.'

'You're joking!' Jade's eyes widened. 'What's wrong with him? Is he not feeling well?' She chuckled as she helped to put away the packages. She was glowing with health, her long, chestnut-coloured hair gleaming like the copper pans that decorated the far wall, touched by the morning sunlight. Her green eyes reflected the happiness that came from being a woman in love and for a second or two Lucy envied her that feeling.

She sighed and brushed those thoughts away. Romance wasn't for her. Not now, not perhaps for some time to come. It was a disappointment, finding out how shallow men could be. Though that wasn't true of all men, of course. Jade's fiancé was a wonderful man. He thought the world of Jade, and they were truly blessed, but it wasn't likely that such a liaison would happen for her any time soon.

Why was it that every time she was halfway interested in a man, he was all over her and trying to hustle her into bed? She didn't want a brief fling based purely on sex, she wanted something more than that—something deeper and more meaningful, a man to love her, perhaps, and care for her, and not just be obsessed by her body. But it wasn't happening. So far, every man she'd met hadn't been able to get past the way she looked. Even Alex, whom she'd known for some years and whom she'd thought at one time might be the one for her, had let her down and left her disappointed.

She tried to shake off those negative feelings. 'I think Matt's on top form lately. I get the feeling he's really happy to be working in Paediatrics, and he doesn't seem to be fazed by anything. One minute he's doing chest drainage on a baby and the next he's playing *Air Attack* with a ten-year-old on the ward. I wish I could be as relaxed about the job.'

Jade nodded. 'It doesn't help that we have clinical examinations coming up next month, does it?'

Lucy gave a slight shudder. 'It's definitely stressful. I've been trying not to think too much about them, but with them looming up ahead there's no avoiding it any longer. I just hope I manage to keep it all together, and that my mind doesn't go blank when the time comes.'

'Me, too.'

'Whose mind's going blank?' Matt joined them in the kitchen, casually dressed in jeans and T-shirt, the cotton fabric hugging his muscular chest and showing off strong, sun-bronzed arms that were covered with a smattering of dark hair. Lucy guessed he'd just come from the shower because his hair was damp and spiky, giving him a roguish, ready-for-anything kind of look.

'Mine,' she told him, and before she could add, 'we were talking about exams,' he started to nod.

'That figures,' he said, his mouth crooking at the corners.

She gave him a soft punch on the arm and he pretended to be wounded. 'Did I say anything about you being an airhead?' he grumbled. 'I mean, just because you forget the groceries occasionally and the cooker still hasn't been repaired, it doesn't have to mean there's nothing going on in there, does it? Anyway, you're blonde…it goes with the territory.'

She scowled at him. 'Don't push it, okay? That joke is wearing a bit thin. I hear it all the time, and I'm telling you I'm not in the mood. As to the cooker, the repairman's coming this morning.'

'That's good. We've only been waiting a week.'

'And that was hardly my fault,' she said in a clipped tone, staying on the defensive. 'I rang several companies, and this was the earliest any-one could come out.'

'Did I say it was your fault?' Matt raised dark brows.

'Okay, children,' Jade interrupted, smiling, 'I'm going to leave you to it. I have a lecture to attend this afternoon, but before that I want to spend some time in the hospital library, looking up clinical exam questions to see what sort of thing might come up.' She glanced at Lucy. 'Are you coming along?'

'I'd like to, but it depends how things go here. I asked the cooker man to come early, but he's al-ready late. I'll catch up with you as soon as I can.'

'See you later, then.' Jade left, and Lucy returned to the task of putting away the last of the packages.

Matt added coffee to the filter jug and said, 'I could wait in for the repairman, if you like. I don't have to be at work until lunchtime today.'

Lucy turned around to look at him, touched by his thoughtfulness. 'Would you? That would be so helpful—I really ought to go to this lecture. It's not quite the same, looking things up on the internet. My head's been all over the place just lately, and a face-to-face meeting is so much better because you can ask questions and clear up niggling difficulties.'

He nodded, but just as she thought about getting ready to leave Matt glanced out of the kitchen window and said softly, 'Well, now, it looks as though we have a visitor. I wonder what that little lad is doing here?' He walked over to the sink to get a better look.

Lucy went to join him at the window, looking out on to the small garden.

'He must be the little boy from next door,' she

said. Matt brushed up against her as he moved to get a better view, and for a while her concentration went to pieces as she stared distractedly at the patch of lawn and surrounding flowers and shrubs.

'He can't even be three years old,' Matt mused, his voice low. 'I wonder how he managed to get into the garden?'

Lucy didn't answer straight away. Matt was so close that she could feel the warmth of his long body seeping into her, and as he lifted an arm to point out a small figure scrambling about in the bushes she was conscious of his biceps lightly grazing the softness of her breast. His thigh was gently pressuring hers, and a rush of heat spread through her, firing up every nerve ending and shooting her nervous system into a spiralling state of heightened awareness.

'I…uh…I think he must have crawled in through a gap in the fence,' she managed, her voice becoming husky.

'Mmm.' Matt half turned, looking at her. 'I expect so.' He sounded distant all at once, and he shifted slightly, so that she wondered if he, too, was overcome by this same feeling of warm intimacy that was bothering her, where her soft curves were brought into mind-shattering contact with his strong, firm body.

'Perhaps I should go and talk to him,' she murmured breathlessly, making an effort to get herself together. 'His mother might be worrying about him.'

'Yes, I think you're right.' He moved away from her, slowly, and it seemed as though his mind was somewhere else altogether. 'I'll come with you.'

They went out through the French doors into the garden, quietly, so as not to startle the little boy. By now, he was sitting on a collection of pebbles that were lit up in a patch of sunlight.

'Hello,' Lucy said softly, bending down to be on a level with the child. 'Are you from next door? I don't think we've met before, have we? I'm Lucy, and this is my friend, Matt.'

'I'm Jacob,' he told her, unperturbed by their sudden appearance. 'I live over there.' He waved an arm towards the fence. 'I've never been here before.' He looked around, his grey eyes bright with curiosity. 'Is this your garden?'

'Yes, it is.' Lucy nodded.

'I like it here.' He pushed his fingers into the pebbles and laughed when the smaller ones fell through his fingers to the ground. 'These are good. If I had my truck, I could fill it up wiv these.'

Matt nodded, kneeling down beside the boy. 'I expect you could. That would be fun, wouldn't it? But perhaps we should find out if your mother knows where you are. She might be worried.'

Jacob shook his head. 'She won't be worried. She's bathing the baby.' He frowned. 'She has to,' he added knowledgeably, 'because she fills her nappy and gets stinky. Babies are like that, aren't they? They're smelly and they cry a lot.'

Matt laughed. 'I suppose so, but they're not like that all the time.'

Jacob screwed up his nose and pursed his pink mouth. Obviously he wasn't too sure about that.

From somewhere in the distance Lucy heard the doorbell ring. 'That'll be the man about the cooker,' she said, glancing worriedly at Matt. 'I ought to go and let him in.'

'Okay. I'll see to it that Jacob gets home all right.'

'Thanks.'

She smiled at the little boy. 'Bye for now, Jacob. I'll probably see you again sometime.'

He nodded cautiously. 'Prob'ly,' he said.

The repairman was nonchalantly looking around when she opened the front door to him, but as soon as he saw her, his eyes widened. He looked her up and down, taking in the clinging, cotton top she was wearing, and the skirt that hugged the line of her shapely hips.

'Um… Domestic oven service. You called our company out because your grill's not working?'

'That's right. I'm so glad you've come.'

He was a good-looking young man, in his mid-twenties or thereabouts, with dark, silky hair that had a natural wave. His glance moved over her once more, and he took a moment to bring his mind back on track before he said with a grin, 'Consider me at your service.'

'Come on in.' She was well used to men look-ing at her that way, so she ignored his stares and showed him into the kitchen. 'It's not lighting up or getting hot or anything,' she told him.

'I'll take a look.'

'Thanks.'

He opened up his kit box and began testing various parts of the cooker. 'Your element's had it,' he said after a while. 'I can fit a new one for you. There's one in my van.'

'Oh, good.' She smiled. 'That's a relief. I won-dered if you might have to send away for the part.' She shrugged. 'I suppose I couldn't expect it to go on working forever. It gets a lot of use, one way and another.'

He nodded. 'They generally do.' He gave her a thoughtful look and said cheerfully, 'The only way round that is to go out for meals. I'd be happy to take you out and free you up from all that cooking…if you're not otherwise engaged, that is?' His glance went to the fingers of her left hand, and when he saw that she wasn't wearing a ring, his confidence seemed to grow. 'There's a new place opened up in the city. I don't know what kind of food you like, but I've heard good things about the restaurant. We could go there this evening, if you like.'

Lucy smiled again, but shook her head. 'Thanks for the invitation, but I'm afraid I've given up on dating. I have other things to concentrate on right now…like my studies and exams.'

His mouth made a wry twist. 'That's a shame,' he said. 'An awful shame. Seems to me we should all take a break every now and again.'

He eyed her up once more before reluctantly leaving her while he went outside to his van. When he came back a short time later, he set to and fixed the new element in place, and then asked if he could wash his hands at the sink.

'Of course, go ahead.' She took a clean towel from a cupboard and handed it to him.

'You know,' he murmured, drying his hands and putting the towel to one side, 'it would be such a pity to give up on the dating game. You're gorgeous, absolutely stunning, in fact, and I can't believe you're content to stay at home and swot every night. Give me half a chance, and I could show you what you're missing.'

She shook her head once more and said lightly, 'Thanks for the offer, but no, thanks…I meant what I said. I'm not going to change my mind. Do you want to give me the bill, and I'll settle up with you?'

He pulled a face and wrote out the invoice, and Lucy handed him a cheque. 'I appreciate you fixing the grill for me,' she said. 'Thanks.'

'You don't need to thank me…just change your mind and come out with me this evening.' He moved a little closer and Lucy took a step backwards.

'I already gave you my answer,' she said firmly. 'I'm sorry, but I can't.'

'Sure you can,' he murmured. 'We'd be great together, you and I. A night on the town would do you a world of good.' He moved towards her once more, but this time Lucy stood her ground.

'I don't think you're listening to me,' she said, her tone brisk, but she was wondering what she ought to do about him. He was certainly persistent. In fact, if he came any closer, she might have to resort to drastic action, something a little more forceful than mere words perhaps since he didn't seem to be taking any notice of what she said.

'I believe she's already given you her answer,' Matt remarked coolly from the doorway. 'Or perhaps you don't understand that "no" means no?'

Lucy was startled. She hadn't heard the kitchen door open, but Matt stood there, broad-shouldered, straight-backed, formidable, his eyes glittering like steel, lancing into the man who was holding on to her.

The young man stared at him in confusion. 'Who are you? Where did you come from?'

'I'm the man who's looking out for her, and I live here. Do you have a problem with that?' He dared him to answer. Matt's jaw was rigid, his mouth set in a hard line that brooked no non-sense. Lucy had never seen him like this before, and she was astonished that the easy-going, laid-back man that she knew had suddenly turned into this granite-edged guardian.

He walked towards them, his long stride steady

and determined. 'It looks as though you've finished your job,' he said, looking at the closed toolbox and the old element on the kitchen worktop. 'Now it's time for you to leave.'

'I... Yes, well, I...' the young man floundered, pulling his hands away from Lucy as though he'd been stung. 'I didn't mean anything by it. I was just asking her out.'

'And you had your answer. Now you should go.'

'Okay, I'm out of here.' He put up his hands in a gesture of submission and then hurriedly grabbed his toolbox. Matt followed him to the door and watched him get into his van and drive away.

Coming back along the corridor to where she was waiting, he glanced at Lucy and said calmly, 'I can't leave you alone for five minutes, can I? Men take one look at you and their brains fly out the window.'

She stared at him, dumbfounded. 'Is that my fault?' she said, feeling affronted. 'Do you think I like it that way? I hate that it always happens. I hate it that other women resent me for the way I look, but I can't do anything about it. I wish I could, but I can't…unless…' Her mind whirled. 'Perhaps I should scrape my hair back into a ponytail and start wearing baggy clothes.'

'I can't see that working,' he said with a wry smile. 'Anyway, I was just teasing you—you make it so easy for me because you always rise to the bait. You really shouldn't take things so seriously, you know.'

She frowned. 'No, maybe not. But just lately I can't help it. I feel as though I'm under pressure all the while, and you have a knack of turning the key and winding me up even more. I don't want to feel that way.' Her gaze flicked to him. 'About what happened with the repairman just now… There was no need for you to intervene, you know. I was handling things. I was perfectly able to deal with him.'

'Sure you were.' He draped an arm around her and led her back towards the kitchen. 'Anyway, forget about it. You have more important things to think about right now, don't you?'

She looked at him in consternation. 'Oh—the lecture, yes. I must get my head clear.' She dithered for a second or two, undecided what she should do first. 'I have to get my bag… And I need to sort out some paperwork for my father before I go—he'll be ringing to ask me about it later today and I need to have it to hand.' She frowned, trying to bring her thoughts into order. 'What happened about the little boy…Jacob? Is he all right? He didn't look as though he wanted to leave, did he?'

She realised that it might seem as though she was babbling, and she stopped talking, her mind in a whirl. Then she put a hand to her head and said raggedly, 'Why can't I think straight? What's wrong with me? I'm not usually like this, and I don't understand it. I don't know what's happening to me.'

'Hmm.' He was thoughtful for a moment or two. 'I think you should sit down for a few minutes before you do anything at all. I'll make you a milky coffee. That will help you to focus. Just try to stay calm for a while—you're always so busy, busy, busy, but I'm sure you don't have to fill every single minute of the day.'

He laid a hand on her shoulder and lightly pressed her down into a chair by the table. And that would have been good, she might have taken comfort in his gentle urging and given herself a few moments to gather her thoughts, except that her mobile phone rang and from the display she saw that it was her father who was calling.

She pulled in a deep breath before answering. 'Hello, Dad, what is it? I thought you were going to ring later. Is everything all right back home?'

'Of course everything's fine. But the work's piling up, and I need you to go and take a look at the house you mentioned to me at the weekend… the one that's coming up for auction. I want to know if the structure is sound. How much work needs to be done? How much is it going to cost me to bring it up to scratch and what price do I bid to make a decent profit? The auction's on Thursday, so you'll need to do it in the next couple of days.'

Her mind reeled at the influx of new instructions. 'I can't, Dad. I can't do anything more than the basics right now. I'm snowed under. Do you remember, I told you I've started my new placement? That means a lot of extra work, and I have exams coming up. I don't have any spare time. I can manage the internet research, but that's about it.'

'You have the evenings, don't you? You can't be studying the whole time.' He sounded affronted. 'Anyway, how long will it take for you to get over there? It's only a hop and a skip away from you.'

'No, but that's not the point, Dad. You're not listening to me. I have exams, and I have to study every chance I get. With the best will in the world I can't go checking out houses right now. This is my career we're talking about—I have to take the time to work at it.'

'You had a career all laid out for you back here in the family business.' His tone was blunt. 'I'm not asking for the world, Lucy, just a few minutes of your time. It's not beyond you to give me that, is it?' His tone was scathing. 'You know I can't get over there right now, with the accountants coming to see me.'

She sighed heavily. It was always the same. He

never listened to her. No matter what she said, he would never understand her point of view. It wasn't important to him. All that mattered to him was the family business, the company that his grandfather had started and had passed on to his son, and which from there had come to him. She felt as though she was being pulled in all directions. She knew he wouldn't back down.

'All right,' she said with a sigh, giving in. 'I'll see what I can do…but I'm making no promises.'

He cut the call, after asking about the paperwork she had prepared for him, and she pushed the phone into her bag, staring into space, her thoughts bleak.

'Well, now we know why your mind is all over the place, don't we?' Matt said, sliding a coffee mug towards her across the table. 'It's the same thing he does with my father. He pushes and pushes and doesn't consider the effect his demands have on other people.'

Lucy winced. 'He's not a bad person. He just has so much drive and energy, and he can't understand why other people don't have the same priorities. I know your father works hard.'

'Too hard.' Matt was grim-faced. 'His team does all the building work for your father, and they're stretched to the limit to keep up with all the projects he's taken on. My father's recruited more men, but even so they can't pull in all the extra work. My mother's worried sick about him. She says he's not sleeping well and she thinks he has the beginnings of a stomach ulcer.'

Her blue eyes were troubled. 'It must be a huge anxiety for her.'

'Yes, it is. For me, too.'

Lucy's shoulders slumped. Was this problem with her father going to drive a wedge between them? She had to share this house with Matt, and she didn't want any bad feelings to blow up between them.

Things had been different a few months ago when the two families had rubbed along well together—after all, it was the sole reason that Matt was living here in the house with Jade, Ben and herself. Her father was very particular about who shared the living accommodation with his daughter, but he had been only too pleased to help out by giving his partner's son a place to live when Matt had been offered a job at the local hospital. But now it looked as though being in business together was going to have all sorts of repercussions, especially if it was no longer an amicable arrangement.

'Drink up.' Matt inclined his head towards her coffee mug. 'Once you get that down you, you should be able to make it to the hospital in time to sort yourself out for this afternoon.' As an afterthought, he added, 'And make sure you eat lunch.'

'I will.' She sipped her coffee and glanced at him over the rim of her cup. 'I almost forgot—what happened with the little boy in the garden? Tell me, did his mother realise he had gone missing?'

He smiled. 'Yes, she came looking for him. She thought he must have gone through the fence after the cat. He's a bit of a tearaway apparently—the boy, I mean, not the cat—and there's probably a smidgin of jealousy going on with the baby. I get the impression he keeps his mother on her toes.'

Lucy nodded. 'It sounds that way. I'd wondered about the white cat that keeps appearing in the garden. I don't think they've lived next door for long. The couple in the house before them went off to live in a detached property.'

She finished off her coffee. 'Thanks for that,' she murmured, getting to her feet. 'I must go.'

She fetched her bag from the worktop and then looked at him once more before she headed for the door. 'I should say thanks for stepping in to help me out earlier. I know you meant well but, as I said, I'm perfectly capable of handling things myself. If he'd come on too strong, I was thinking about kneeing him in the groin, but I'm not altogether sure how that would have gone down.'

'Ouch!'

'Yeah!' She gave him a light wave of the hand and left the house, stepping out into the morning sunshine. The trees were in blossom all the way along the crescent, and a good many of the houses were decorated with brightly blooming hanging baskets. It was a glorious summer's day, but something was bothering her and, try as she may, she couldn't quite place what it was.

She walked along the street, ignoring the interested glance of the man who lived across the way. She was used to being avidly watched by the opposite sex wherever she went, and she did her best not to pay any attention. She frowned. Perhaps that was the source of what was playing on her mind.

Living together as closely as they did, Matt had never made a pass at her, and before today he'd hardly ever commented on the way she looked. Of course, she was pleased about that because it made life so much easier...but a perverse little imp was prodding and poking her, and prompting her to wonder about it.

Could it be that Matt saw beyond the superficial appearance and found that what was left was ultimately flawed? In his eyes she was her father's daughter, programmed to do his bidding, sometimes a little resentful of that but happy all the same to live on the proceeds of his wealth.

It was a disturbing thought.

CHAPTER THREE

'YOU look worried, Matt. Is anything wrong?' Lucy had come from the neonatal unit and was on her way back to the children's ward when she saw Matt waiting by the main entrance of the hospital. He was frowning, glancing occasionally at his watch and looking out through the glass doors towards the car park.

He shook his head. 'Not really. I'm waiting for my father. He has an appointment with the cardiologist this afternoon, and I want to make sure he's okay. I said I would meet him here and take him over to the department.'

Shocked, she looked at him in dismay. 'I'm so sorry.' She moved closer to him, laying a hand on his forearm in sympathy. 'I didn't realise things had come to that state. Has his condition become much worse?'

'Yes, it seems like it. He's had chest pains for some time, but now they're getting quite bad, and his blood pressure is too high, despite the GP giving him ACE inhibitors to bring it down. I've been working on him whenever I've had the chance to get him to go and see a specialist. His GP was happy to go along with that, but my father wasn't keen at all.' He pulled a face. 'He's always been a proud, strong man, never one to make a fuss. I'm pretty sure the only reason he's coming here at all today is to put my mother's mind at rest.'

A twinge of guilt tightened her chest. Had all this come about because of her father putting pressure on him? She said quietly, 'It's good that you're here to take care of him, anyway. Is your mother coming with him today? It's a bit far out of their way, isn't it?' It was odd that they hadn't opted to go to a hospital in Berkshire, where they had lived for the last forty or so years, but perhaps this hospital's reputation had been the deciding factor.

He nodded. 'That's true. It'll take them about

an hour to get here, but they think it's worth it. We have a first-class reputation for Cardiology at this hospital, which helped sway his mind and, I think, when my father finally agreed, he wanted to be seen here because he knew I'd be near at hand to advise him.'

'Who is the consultant he'll be seeing?'

'Mr Sheldon.' He gave her a thoughtful look. 'You were on placement with him a few weeks ago, weren't you?'

She smiled. 'Yes. He kept me on my toes, but he's a brilliant doctor. I'm sure your father will be in safe hands.'

'Let's hope so. I've had a lot of input, persuading my father to do this, and I'm keeping my fingers crossed that everything will turn out all right.'

Lucy felt for him in his anxiety and she wished there was something she could say that would give him some comfort, but only an all-clear from the specialist would achieve that. The way things were, it didn't look as though that would be forthcoming.

Looking down, she realised that she was still holding on to his arm, and now she self-consciously let her hand fall to her side. His body was tense, the muscles of his arms rigid, and she wished she could do more than just sympathise.

'Will you let me know how he gets on?' she said. 'I have to go and look at a patient for Professor Farnham so I'll be on the children's ward for the rest of the morning. Good luck with your father.'

He acknowledged that with a nod and she left him, walking over to the lift bay, heading for Paediatrics. It bothered her, somehow, that Matt was looking so serious. It wasn't like him—he was usually so laid-back and calm—but it just went to show how concerned he was for his father's well-being.

Back on the children's ward, she went to check up on the baby who had been suffering from pneumonia, along with a pleural infection.

'Well, isn't he looking better?' she said, her mouth curving in delight as she came across the young mother, who was holding her son tenderly on her lap. The infant gurgled and gave Lucy a toothy smile. She let him grasp her fingers with his tiny fist, and asked, 'Do you think I could have a listen to your chest, young man?'

The baby seemed happy enough to oblige, allowing his mother to lift his vest so that Lucy could run the stethoscope carefully over his chest. After a minute or so she pushed the stethoscope back down into her pocket and said in a cheerful tone, 'That sounds good. It shouldn't be too long before he's able to go home.'

His mother beamed with relief, and Lucy left them a short time later and went to check up on the ten-year-old boy who had been admitted a few days ago after a traffic accident. His parents had also been injured in the accident, but they had been discharged after a couple of days, and now their child was their sole concern. He had been admitted with a spleen injury, and the professor was giving him supportive treatment, keeping an eye on the situation because he preferred not to operate if it was at all possible.

'How are you feeling today, William?' she

asked. He was very pale and unusually subdued, and immediately she was on the alert.

He tried to sit up, but collapsed back against the pillows. 'I feel sick,' he muttered, and Lucy hurriedly reached for a kidney bowl and handed it to him.

'Breathe deeply, if you can, and try to stay still,' she told him. 'I'll just check your blood pressure, and see if we can find out what's happening.' She glanced at him as she wrapped the blood-pressure cuff around his arm.

'Did this come on suddenly?'

He nodded, and said briefly, 'After I got out of bed to go to the toilet.'

Lucy frowned. That hadn't caused him too many problems before, so what had been differ-ent about this time?

'Were you on your feet for longer than usual?'

He managed a sheepish half smile. 'I went to play with some of the toys across the other side of the ward.' Talking exhausted him and he closed his eyes.

'Until the nurse found him and shooed him

back to bed,' his mother finished for him. 'He's
not been well since then. I'd gone to get a cup
of coffee, or I'd have stopped him. He's always
been too lively for his own good.'

Lucy acknowledged that with a smile. Of
course most children, especially boys, were naturally adventurous, and could stray into trouble
from time to time. She kept her thoughts hidden,
but she was worried about the drop in the boy's
blood pressure and his increased heart rate. His
pulse was weak. Put together, they added up to
signs of imminent shock.

'I just want to examine your tummy, William,'
she said. 'I'll be as gentle as possible.'

Even so, it was clear that he was in pain, and his
abdomen was distended, which made her even
more concerned. There was an area of bruising
under his ribcage on the left side, in the region of
his spleen, plus another, more recent, reddened
patch.

'Did you bump into something when you got
out of bed?' she asked quietly.

He pressed his lips together, and she guessed

he was unwilling to answer so she said quickly, 'You're not in any kind of trouble. It's all right to tell me.'

'I tried to climb up on a chair to reach something, but I felt dizzy and slipped and banged myself on the seat.' Breathless, he fell silent once more and after a few seconds he began to retch.

His mother helped him with the kidney dish and silently sucked in her breath while Lucy quickly jotted down her findings on his chart. Everything was becoming clear to her now. Wasn't it likely that the fall would have been the cause of his problems? An injury coming on top of an already damaged spleen could have been the final straw, causing an increase in the internal bleeding from the initial injury, to such an extent that now it looked as though blood was building up inside his abdominal cavity. If she was right, this was extremely bad news—an emergency situation. Too much blood loss could be fatal.

'All right, sweetheart,' she murmured, keeping her tone calm and pacifying. 'I'll get the doctor to come and look at you and we'll make sure you're feeling better soon.' Turning to his mother, she said, 'He needs to rest completely, and lying back with a couple of pillows under his legs might be best. I'll be back in a minute or two.'

She moved away from the side of the bed, debating what to do next. What if she was wrong in her diagnosis and there was some other interpretation to be drawn from his symptoms? Even so, she sent out urgent pager messages calling for Matt and the professor to come and look at the patient, and then she went to find Mandy, the nurse in charge of the ward.

Mandy was startled to hear about the change in William's condition. 'He was fine just half an hour ago,' she said. 'I found him playing with the train set and took him back to his bed. I felt bad about doing that, but he's supposed to have complete bed rest—Professor Farnham's orders.'

She was a pretty young woman, fair haired, with a delicate rose-bloom complexion, and she was also very good at her job. Lucy had learned to rely on her in the short time she'd been working in Paediatrics. 'The professor's in an important meeting,' Mandy commented. 'He didn't want to be disturbed. Perhaps we ought to bring in the registrar, instead.'

Lucy winced. 'It's too late. I've already paged him, and Matt, too. Anyway, the registrar is busy with a baby in Neonatal. A three-week-old baby suffered a cardiac arrest this morning and he's trying to find out what caused it.' She pressed her lips together as she fought off her doubts. 'Don't worry. I'll take the flak if there's a problem. I was the one who decided it was important enough to fetch the professor out.'

Matt came on to the ward as she and Mandy were assessing the boy's vital signs once more. 'Something going on here?' he asked in a soft voice. He studied the monitors and then glanced at Lucy. 'Those readings don't look too good.'

'No, they don't.' By now, it looked as though the boy was going rapidly downhill, and she hurriedly explained the situation while Matt made a brief but thorough examination of the child.

'His pulse is weak and thready—he's going into shock,' Matt said. 'We need to get him stabilised.' He went into immediate action, putting in a fluid line to compensate for the blood loss and giving the boy oxygen.

'He'll have to go for emergency surgery, won't he?' Lucy asked. 'I wondered whether to alert Theatre, but decided against it. I thought, being a student, I might be presuming too much, especially if the professor was to arrive at any minute.'

'I'll do it,' Matt said. 'And I'll call for a surgeon to be on standby in case the professor is delayed. I don't think there'll be time for a CT scan. He could bleed out before it's finished unless we act quickly. We have to get the mother to sign a consent form.'

Lucy pulled in a deep breath. So it was every bit as bad as she'd feared, and now it was down to her to explain things to the mother while Matt and Mandy worked to prepare the boy for surgery.

William's mother was shocked by the seriousness of the situation. 'Will he have to have his spleen removed?' she asked, almost in a whisper so that her son wouldn't hear what was being said. 'That would be really bad, wouldn't it?'

'We won't know for sure what's going to happen until the surgeon has him up in Theatre, I'm afraid. If it's at all possible, he'll try to repair the spleen and stop the bleeding. You're right, the spleen is an important organ because it helps us to guard against infection, but if it has to be removed it means that we'll need to be sure William is always kept up to date with his vaccinations, and he may need antibiotics on occasions to prevent him becoming ill.' She waited for Mrs Bradshaw to absorb all that, and then added, 'I know this must be a worrying time for you, but we'll keep you informed all the way through. Don't be afraid to ask any questions. We'll be glad to answer them.'

By now, Professor Farnham had arrived on the ward, and quickly sized up the situation. 'I'll go and scrub in for surgery,' he said, with a nod towards Lucy. 'Well spotted.'

She was glad of the small words of praise, but they didn't really make her feel any better. All she could think of was that small, vulnerable boy, sedated now and being wheeled away towards Theatre, his life hanging in the balance.

She left Mrs Bradshaw with Mandy and went in search of Matt. He was in the doctors' writing-up area, adding notes to the boy's computer file, but he finished typing and turned around to look at her as she approached.

'It was a good thing you acted when you did,' he said. He shook his head. 'It's hard to think I was playing computer games with him just the other day. I don't know how the parents cope. It must be such a shock when something bad like that happens to your child.'

'Yes…although I don't suppose you have any choice but to keep going and keep doing your best for them.' Her gaze was troubled as she thought back to how rapidly the boy's condition had deteriorated. 'I think that's partly why I decided to study medicine, because I saw that doctors could make a difference in people's lives. It seemed to me to be a much more worthwhile thing to do than anything else.'

He nodded. 'I feel much the same. I actually thought about specialising in A and E at one time, but I'm still divided between that and Paediatrics.' He gave a faint smile and sent her a thoughtful, assessing look. 'Mandy told me how you kept your cool,' he said. 'She thought you were brilliant.'

She felt a warm rush of pleasure flow through her at his words. 'That's good to know, though I can't say I felt all that confident,' she admitted. 'I kept wondering whether I was overstepping the mark, and I thought maybe I had things wrong, and I shouldn't really be calling the professor to come in.' She perched on the edge of the desk, crossing one long leg over the other without thinking until she noticed his blue gaze glide slowly from the tip of her pale suede kitten heels all the way up to the golden curve of her thigh where it met the taut hem of her skirt.

It was too late to undo the action. Her cheeks flushed with heat and she tried not to notice the spark of flame that kicked into life in the depths of the suddenly darkened eyes that were watching her. It didn't mean anything. It was a trick of the light, wasn't it? After all, this was Matt. He didn't pay any attention to the way she looked, did he? He was more likely to notice that she hadn't got around to emptying the washing machine, or that she was spending an indulgently long time in the bathroom. Not that he ever complained about any of those things…it was just that he had a way of teasing her about them.

She sent him an oblique glance. 'I paged you, but I wasn't sure whether you would be coming on to the ward today. I know you had some study time this morning, and of course you were with your father this afternoon. I didn't know if I would be disturbing you at a bad time.'

'It was okay.' He shrugged. 'The boy had to come first, anyway, whatever I was involved with, but as it happens I was already on my way back to the ward. My parents are on their way home by now.'

'Oh, I see.' He was perfectly relaxed, back to his calm, easy-going self, and she couldn't help but marvel at how well he adapted to different situations.

He had given no sign that anything was troubling him when he had come on to the ward, but had sprung into action straight away, assisting the child, notifying the theatre staff and arranging a surgical consultation.

'How did your father get on this afternoon?' she asked.

'Okay, but he has to go for more tests. Mr Sheldon suspects he has angina, so in the meantime he's given him a nitro spray to use whenever the pain comes on.' His expression became serious once more, his mouth flattened into a grim line.

'I'm sorry.' It was clear that he was still concerned about his father's condition, and she felt awkward about it because she knew in his mind he must be attaching blame and laying it squarely at her father's feet. 'I suppose he must have been ill for some time—I mean, these things don't come on suddenly without warning, do they?' It couldn't be entirely her father's fault, could it?

'I dare say…though my mother had a lot to say on that subject.' The clatter of teatime trolleys sounded in the corridor, and he glanced at his watch. 'It's time I was off duty,' he announced. 'What about you—you're about finished here, aren't you? Are you thinking of going straight home?'

She shook her head. 'I can't. I have to go and look over a property for my father. He mentioned it on the phone the other day. It's coming up for auction and he wants to know whether to go ahead and put in a bid for it. I'm supposed to suss out the condition of the place and find out what work needs doing.' She frowned. 'I know it's my turn to cook today, but I'll probably be late getting back. I've made sure there's meat and salad in the fridge, so you can all help yourselves.'

'I don't think Jade and Ben will be back for supper today,' he said. She raised a questioning brow, and he added, 'Ben told me they're going to start work on laying new floors, back at their house.' He gave a wry grin. 'I think they'll be making do with a Chinese takeaway.'

'That's your favourite food, isn't it, next to pizza?' She gave him an answering smile. 'Though now I come to think of it, you'll scoff pretty much anything that's going, won't you?'

He lifted his shoulders in a negligent way and she studied him for a moment or two. For all he had a good appetite, his whole body was trim, with not a spare ounce of fat anywhere, as far as she could tell. Perhaps that was because he was always on the move, always up to something or other. He was well muscled, broad shouldered, with a chest that tapered to a lean, flat stomach.

Her gaze wandered to his face. Come to think of it, he was incredibly good-looking, with a strong, angular jaw and a well-shaped, perfect mouth. She specially liked his mouth, that way he had of making a crooked smile, and he would gaze at you with those blue, all-seeing eyes and…

She looked away, heat rippling through her like a tidal wave. What was she doing, letting her thoughts wander like this? Where had all this come from? She was at work, for heaven's sake, and she ought to be behaving in a professional manner, instead of getting carried away with increasingly intimate thoughts about her housemate.

She slid down from the table, tugging on her skirt as she straightened up, and hoped Matt wouldn't have noticed anything amiss.

'Where is this house that you're going to see?' he asked. 'Is it close by?'

'About half an hour away on the train. It's a waterfront property on a small island on the Thames. I think that's what made me notice it on the internet. It sounded like an idyllic situation and perhaps I was a little carried away when I mentioned it to my father.' She winced. 'Anyway, I have to go and take a look, because the auction's coming up the day after tomorrow. I just hope I don't get it wrong and pitch the target price too low or underestimate how much work needs doing.'

'Would you like me to go with you? For moral support, I mean.'

She blinked, startled by his suggestion. 'Would you mind doing that? I mean—' she floundered for a second or two '—it might take quite a while to look around, if I'm to do a proper job.'

'I don't mind at all. In fact, I'd quite like to see something of how your father operates. I know he has developments going on all over the place, large and small, but this will give me an insight into how one tiny part of the business works.' His glance flicked over her. 'Besides, I thought you might like some company. You've been under a lot of pressure lately, and I know this is one more thing you could do without. Perhaps if you have someone to share it with, it won't feel so bad.'

'I… Yes, you're right. Thank you. I'd like that.' She was touched by his concern. She was seeing Matt in a new light these days. Since they'd been plunged into working together on a daily basis, she was learning so much more about him than she had in all the months they'd been living under the same roof.

He surprised her with his comments, though. She'd had no idea he was interested in the business but perhaps, with his father being ill, it was uppermost in his mind right now. 'Doesn't your father talk to you about his work?' she asked, curious. 'I mean, he's in partnership with my dad, so you must get some idea of what goes on.'

He stood up, and they walked together along the corridor towards the exit. 'Of course, but my father operates the building and actual development side of things. He doesn't choose which properties are going to be renovated or which sites are ripe for development. I guess he must have an opinion from time to time, but it's not his main priority.'

'No, I suppose you're right.' They went out of the Paediatric unit and headed for the main doors.

'I wish we knew more about how young William was getting on,' she said as they left the hospital. 'If I wasn't so pushed for time, I'd have stayed on to see him come out of Theatre.'

He nodded. 'I feel much the same way, but we can ring up in an hour or so to find out what's happening. We're not going to do much good waiting around, and it's pretty certain that as soon as he's out of the recovery room he'll be taken to the intensive-care unit. He's in good hands with the professor, anyway.'

They walked along the London streets towards the station, bathed in the late afternoon sunshine. It dappled the leaves on the trees that lined the thoroughfare, and Lucy felt the warmth of it on her bare arms. All the time she was conscious of Matt by her side, tall, long limbed, fitting his pace to hers.

Entering the station was like stepping into another world, cool, relatively noisy, full of busy people intent on making their way home. After a few minutes they boarded the train that would take them to their destination, and Matt slid an arm around her waist to shield her from the buffeting crowd.

It was a natural gesture, and it felt surprisingly good to have him hold her. She wasn't used to feeling this way about Matt, being at ease with him, sharing the everyday simple task of getting to and from work. It was a comfortable, pleasurable feeling, as though he was lifting some of the stress from her, and for the first time in a long while she began to relax.

They left the train about half an hour later, and walked the rest of the way, crossing a footbridge over the Thames to access the island.

'It's a very small island,' Lucy said, looking around, 'but there are about fifty houses on it. Apparently lots of people want to come and live here, so when a property comes up for sale, there's a lot of interest.' She frowned, thinking about that.

'Do you think your father might be put off by that?' Matt was watching her, gauging her expression.

'It's possible. It would push the price up.'

'And that bothers you?'

She pondered that for a moment or two. 'Yes, I think so. Somehow I would hate to miss out on the opportunity to buy a house in this area. It feels so—' she looked around '—tranquil here. I can't help thinking it would be good to come here at the end of the day, away from noise and hassle, and just steep yourself in this picturesque place and breathe in the fresh air.'

He chuckled. 'Sounds like you're a country girl at heart.'

She nodded, laughing with him. 'You probably have something there. It comes from being brought up in the Berkshire countryside, I suppose... All those green meadows and wooded hillsides. A little bit of me wishes I was still there, and this backwater—' she waved a hand towards the gently flowing river, with its lush green banks dotted with trees whose branches swayed in the soft breeze '—seems to fill that gap somehow.'

'You're personalising it,' he commented. 'The house won't be yours, and, anyway, you haven't seen it yet.' He walked with her, and together they checked the map to see which property was up for sale. 'It might be completely dilapidated and beyond repair—not such a haven after all.'

'Maybe.'

They found it some five minutes later, overlooking the waterway, a detached house, white-painted, with dormer windows and a lower, gabled extension.

'Oh, it's beautiful,' Lucy said, gazing at the house in awe. 'Imagine sitting out here on a summer's day, looking out over the river. It even has its own mooring and slipway.' She frowned and studied the paper that gave the details of the property. 'It says some of the rooms require attention.' She glanced at Matt. 'That could mean anything, couldn't it, from a quick splash of paint to a complete refit?'

'True. Let's go and find out, shall we?'

They went into the house and wandered through the rooms, and Lucy tried her best to look at them objectively, sizing them up and noting down the things her father needed to know. It was hard to keep a clear mind on the subject, though, because deep down she knew she had already fallen in love with the place.

'The fireplace will need replacing in here,' Matt said, looking around the living room. 'And the kitchen could do with a refit.'

'Yes, but look at that view,' Lucy pointed out,

her voice tinged with excitement. 'How could anyone not be smitten by that landscape? Two whole walls of glass and a terrace where you can sit out and while away the hours. I can just imagine myself living here.'

'As if you have time to sit around. Being a doctor means shift work and ongoing study to keep up to date, and crawling into bed dog-tired.' Matt was smiling, taking in her absorbed expression, but even his gentle teasing couldn't bring her down to earth.

'You won't spoil it for me, no matter what you say,' she told him, shaking her head. 'It's cast a spell on me, and I'm hooked.'

'So much so that you forget your father will sell it on to someone else. What are you going to do, come and press your face up against the glass every now and again and mourn what you can't have?'

'Oh, you're such a spoilsport,' she said, turning to look at him. 'I'm not going to listen to you.'

'I didn't think you would,' he said, his mouth making a crooked line. His tone softened. 'I just don't want to see you hurt, that's all. Even you wouldn't be able to persuade your father to hang on to it. And you're not in the market for buying, are you?'

'I can dream, can't I?' She frowned, then turned away from him and went to open the patio doors and gaze out at the tree-lined bank opposite. She wouldn't let him burst her bubble. She wouldn't.

She sat on a bench on the terrace and jotted down everything that she'd observed. 'A golden oak kitchen,' she said, making a quick sketch, 'with an island hob and a range cooker set into the recess, and maybe an overhanging fixture for copper pans.' She scribbled some more. 'A tiled work surface—and upstairs we'd need to build in wardrobes and add an en suite bathroom to the main bedroom.'

'How about a new fireplace for the living room?' Matt suggested. 'A proper open grate with coals that look like the real thing.'

She nodded. 'Good idea. What about the floors? Tiles in the kitchen, or wood?'

He smiled. 'Wood throughout—honey-coloured oak, to give the feeling of warmth in the winter.'

She looked at him. 'You're good at this sort of thing, aren't you? Have you been practising? Are you thinking of buying a place of your own?' It was her turn to tease him now. He'd always seemed content to live in their Georgian terrace, close to the hospital where he worked. And though he got on well with lots of young women, she didn't think there was anyone special in his life right now, so why would he be thinking of settling down in his own place?

'You never know,' he said, taking her by surprise. 'I can't live in rented property for evermore.'

'No, of course not.' She hoped her feelings didn't show. It would be so strange not to have him living with them at the house. She was so used to his half awake, half asleep appearance in the kitchen each morning, his constant strumming on the guitar that caused her to glower at him occasionally when she was trying to concentrate on something. But how would she feel if he was no longer there? The house would be empty without him. *She* would be empty, somehow, drifting, like a boat that had lost its rudder.

She blinked and tried to push those thoughts out of her mind. He wouldn't leave. He had no reason to go...not yet, did he?

CHAPTER FOUR

LUCY walked into the neonatal unit and glanced around, conscious of a sense of anxiety weighing her down. She'd been in Paediatrics all morning, but every so often she was scheduled to work in Neonatal, and this afternoon was one of those occasions. She had mixed feelings about spending time in here, because all of the patients were incredibly small and hugely dependent on the care of the doctors and nurses and on all the complicated equipment that helped to keep them alive.

She brightened a little when she saw Matt at the far side of the room. Somehow his presence made her feel more confident, more at ease with the highly specialised nature of the department where she was just a minor cog. He was a friendly face amidst all this uncertainty.

He was looking after one of the babies, setting up a feeding tube and checking that all was well, but even so, he took time to acknowledge her with a smile and a nod of his head.

She waved back, then went over to the desk and glanced through the patients' files until she found the one she was looking for.

'Hi, there.' James Tyler, the registrar, came to stand beside her, greeting her with a cheerful smile. 'How are things with you? I saw you in the library with Jade at lunchtime, working at the computer. It won't be too long before you two take your final clinical exams, will it?'

'Oh, don't remind me!' A host of emotions flickered across Lucy's face as she thought about all the studying she still had to get through, and the battle she had with finding the time to fit it all in. She still had to figure out the costs involved if her father was to put in a bid for the house she and Matt had gone to view yesterday. 'I'm trying to take things one step at a time. If I look at everything I still have to do, I'll start to panic.'

He shook his head. 'You have to remember to take time out to relax and recharge your batteries.

That way you'll be able to cope so much better. You're a conscientious, intelligent young woman, and I'm sure you already know far more than you think. The studying is all extra refinement.'

She laughed. 'If only that were true!'

He laid a hand on her waist, an intimate gesture that made her feel slightly uncomfortable. She liked James, but not in the way that he would prefer. 'It is,' he persisted, 'I'm sure of it. And I'm serious about the relaxation bit. Why don't we get together, just you and I, this evening and find a cosy bar overlooking the Thames? Maybe one that has music. It'll do you a world of good to get out and about and forget about work and your studies for a while.'

They'd been here before, and she wondered how she could once again let him down lightly. She hesitated for a second or two, and then said, 'Thanks, James, it sounds like a lovely idea, but you know it's not on, don't you? Like I've said before, I've been down the dating route and it wasn't a good experience. I'm not looking to put my toe in the water again for a while, especially when there are so many other things going on in my life right now.'

He didn't seem to be too put out by what she had said. Instead, she guessed with a feeling of growing frustration that his mind was busy working on a counter-argument.

His gaze moved over her, lingering on the golden hair that fell in a shimmering cloud to her shoulders. 'But you and I would be different. I know it. We get on so well together, we share the same interests… You like the countryside, reading, exploring new places…'

She shook her head. 'I'm sorry, but I can't. I'm sure that going to the pub would be a great evening out—why don't you ask Alice to go with you? I know she enjoys live music.' Alice was the nurse in charge of Neonatal, pretty and dark haired, who put all her energy into the job and worked magic with her young charges. 'She could do with some fun in her life.'

'And Lucy can listen to music every day if she wants,' Matt cut in, coming over to the desk. Tall, fit-looking and vitally energetic, he looked completely at ease in this highly specialised environment. 'She knows I'll be only too glad to play her a tune on my guitar any time she likes.' He tossed a file into the wire tray. 'I do happen to be working on a new song for the students' union disco.' He glanced at Lucy. 'You'd love to hear me practise, wouldn't you, Lucy?'

She rolled her eyes heavenward. 'Uh…if you say so,' she murmured. It was an ongoing bone of contention between them that he strummed his guitar when she was trying to relax or when she was struggling to master a revision topic for her exams. She'd threatened to pull the plug on his amplifier more than once.

James pulled a face, realising that the conversation was over once Matt had joined them. He let his arm slip from her waist. 'I have to go and meet Professor Farnham,' he said, 'so you're in charge, Matt, while I'm away. Perhaps you'd check up on baby Sarah? I persuaded her parents to go outside for a while and get some fresh air, so it gives us a good opportunity to see to her without worrying them.'

'Okay. I'll make her my priority.'

James left the unit, and Matt sent Lucy a thoughtful glance. 'I had the feeling you needed a get-out just then. Was I right, or did I mess things up for you?'

She exhaled slowly. She hadn't realised until then how she'd been holding her breath, keeping a tight rein on her emotions. 'I was hoping he might get the message. I like him, but I'm just not in the mood for going out and living it up right now.'

'Mmm, I got that. Did you mean it when you said dating had been a bad experience for you?'

She nodded. 'It wasn't always that way, but the last time I let my guard down I ended up being trampled. I was hurt pretty badly. I suppose I'm just not keen for that to happen again any time soon.'

'That's understandable.' He studied her curiously. 'I'm surprised anyone would do anything to upset you, though. Most men would be glad just to have won your interest.'

She pressed her lips together briefly, a frown

line working its way into her brow. 'Maybe, but I think it's sometimes better that I don't acknowledge their interest,' she admitted, 'because some men see it as a green light and start an all-out campaign to try to hustle me into bed, whereas, to my mind, I was just trying to be friendly.' Being the focus of male attention was something she lived with, something she was used to by now. 'I want to be appreciated for who I am,' she said, 'not just for my vital statistics.'

He laughed. 'You're probably on a loser there.' He started to walk away from the desk. 'Let's go and take a look at baby Sarah, shall we?' he said.

'Okay.'

She went over to the bay where little Sarah Montgomery lay quietly in an incubator, her stick-thin arms and legs moving restlessly.

Lucy slid her hand into the opening of the incubator and stroked the baby's arm, loving the feel of her downy, soft skin. 'How's she doing?' she asked in a low voice, sending an oblique glance towards Matt. This was the baby that James had been caring for in the Neonatal unit since yesterday morning. She'd been admitted after her heart had stopped and her lips had turned a bluish colour.

'Things aren't looking too good for her, I'm afraid.' Matt was checking the baby's fluid line, but now he stopped for a moment to study the infant. 'She was born prematurely and she's been through an awful lot in these first three weeks of her life. When her heart stopped she wasn't getting enough oxygen, and that could have disastrous consequences. There's a risk of brain damage—always supposing she survives.'

'She's still putting up a fight, though, isn't she?' Lucy's heart went out to this tiny girl. After she'd had a second cardiac arrest in a short space of time James had ordered a CT scan and the results were alarming. There was bleeding in the brain, and that was devastating news for the parents, who were already trying to come to terms with their baby's collapse. 'What caused all these problems, do we know? Is it all down to being born before her proper time?'

'I would think so.' Matt checked the infusion

pump and then noted down the baby's vital signs on a chart. 'The blood vessels in a premature baby's brain are fragile and they can bleed easily. It's hard to say what will happen.' A muscle in his jaw flickered, and Lucy could see that he was disturbed by the baby's vulnerable state. 'There's no treatment we can give her to stop the bleeding. All we can do is hope that the situation will resolve itself. We'll keep her on the ventilator to make sure she's getting enough oxygen, and provide support with fluids and medication to stabilise her blood pressure. It all depends how strong she is as to how things will turn out.'

'Her parents are in bits,' Lucy commented, trailing her little finger down to the baby's hand and gently brushing her tiny fingers. 'Professor Farnham tried to prepare her parents for what might happen, but it must be unbearable for them to see her like this.'

'You'd do best not to think about it, if you possibly can,' Matt warned her. 'Paediatrics and Neonatal are difficult specialties—rewarding, in a lot of ways, but they can be harrowing, as well.'

'I know.' Lucy reluctantly withdrew her hand from the incubator and straightened up. She sighed. 'I know you're right...but it's hard to stay unemotional. Almost impossible, I'd say.'

He nodded. 'You get too involved with your patients for your own good. I saw how anxious you looked when you came back from the intensive-care unit this morning. You went over there to see William, didn't you?'

She hadn't realised he'd noticed her. 'Yes. I was hoping there might be some good news, but he looked so poorly, lying there with all sorts of tubes attached to him and monitors bleeping.' Her expression was bleak. 'I don't know quite what I'd expected, but something a bit more encouraging, perhaps.'

Matt laid an arm around her shoulders. 'At least he came through his operation without having his spleen removed,' he remarked. 'That's something to be thankful for.'

She nodded. He was trying to cheer her up, and she was grateful for that, but when she'd gone along to the intensive-care unit first thing to look in on the boy, she'd been shocked by how white-faced he appeared. Perhaps his peaky, thin face and fair hair emphasised his pallor. He wasn't out of the woods yet, by any means, and he'd been too ill to take much notice of what had been going on around him. He'd lost a lot of blood, and although Professor Farnham had managed to repair his spleen it was a worrying time for everyone as they tried to stabilise his condition.

Matt lightly squeezed her shoulder and then moved away from her to go and write notes on the infant's medication chart. She watched him walk away. She didn't like to admit it, even to herself, but she missed that comforting arm that he'd wrapped around her. She missed the close-ness. For just a little while it had made her feel warm and cherished, but now she was alone once more. She didn't know why that bothered her so much, or why she was so aware of Matt's near-ness these days, but things were changing, she was changing, and for some reason her emotions were all over the place.

Maybe she was simply tired and overwrought.

She'd studied all through her lunch break, taking bites from a sandwich at the computer when the librarian han't been looking. And now that she was due to finish work for the day, she would return home to study some more.

Jade walked with her from the hospital, back to the neat, Georgian house that they all shared. 'I shall be glad when exams are over,' she said. 'The written papers were bad enough, but now there's the practical session to get through. I hate the thought of having to think on my feet and have someone watch me and judge my performance.'

'Me, too. Except that it happens every day, one way or another,' Lucy pointed out. 'I suppose the only difference is that we're not being allocated formal marks for what we do on the wards.'

They arrived home, and Lucy ran the vacuum cleaner around the living areas while Jade disappeared into her room. When she had finished tidying up and seeing to the laundry, Lucy glanced through the paperwork she needed to prepare for her father, and then she, too, went upstairs to revise for her upcoming exams.

She heard Ben and Matt come home an hour later, and after a while, appetising smells began to drift up from the kitchen. It seemed such a long time since lunch. Her mouth watered in anticipation, but she pushed thoughts of food to one side and tried to concentrate instead on the information she was reading on the computer screen. It was Matt's turn to cook this evening. He usually produced straightforward, wholesome meals, anything that could be dished up quickly and without fuss, and his specialty was pizza, with all kinds of different toppings. Today's offering didn't smell like pizza, though.

She tried to shake off those thoughts and dragged her attention back to her studies. It was vital that she go on with her work, and she immersed herself in the lecture notes on screen. She was vaguely aware of hearing Matt's voice a while later, but by then she was deep into learning about things that could go wrong with the renal system. When he shouted up the stairs a few minutes later to say that the meal was ready, she was still engrossed in kidney transplantation and found it hard to prise herself away. Just a minute or two more, and she would be done.

There was a sharp rap on her door some time later, making her jump. 'Are you decent in there?' Matt said in a brisk tone.

'I… Yes…' She frowned, trying to gather her thoughts after the sudden interruption. 'Why?'

He opened the door and glowered at her. 'Because I called you ten minutes ago and, much as I hate to tell you what to do, I can't abide to see good food wasted. If you're not downstairs in two minutes flat, you'll find your dinner inside next door's cat.'

She laughed. 'Yeah, yeah…you wouldn't give your prize concoctions to our furry friend.'

'Wouldn't I? Try me. What's the betting he absolutely loves paella, drools over it, in fact. All that fluffy saffron rice, golden fried chicken, perfectly cooked prawns…?' He was halfway down the stairs when she heard him calling softly, 'Here, kitty, kitty, kitty…'

'No…no,' she shrieked, shutting off the com-

puter and springing to her feet to tear after him.
'You wouldn't dare!'

'Oh, no?' he called back. He was holding her
dinner plate aloft when she arrived, breathless,
in the kitchen. He was already on his way to the
kitchen door. 'Oh, he's going to love this.'

'You do, and I'll…I'll…' She searched her brain
to find something suitably heinous. 'My red top
will find its way into your laundry,' she threatened.

'Now, that would be a mistake,' he said, smiling, giving her plate a twirl as he turned to face
her from the kitchen door. 'I know where you
keep the bleach, you see, and you really wouldn't
like to see that pretty red top all patchy and sorry
looking, would you?'

'Children, children!' Jade cut in, looking on
and laughing. 'Settle down. If you two don't sit
down and finish your meals like good kiddies,
you'll find yourselves doing the washing up.'

'That's a warning and a half,' Ben said with
a grin. 'Just look at all those pans that need
cleaning.' His grey-blue eyes sparkled. 'Carry

on, if you like. I really wasn't looking forward to doing them.'

Matt slid the dinner plate onto the kitchen table. 'Saved in the nick of time,' he said, giving Lucy a triumphant smile. 'Sit. Eat. Be thankful I kept it hot for you.'

He slid into his seat at the table and dipped a spoon into his dessert, a beautifully whipped concoction of strawberry mousse, topped with luscious, fresh strawberries.

Lucy sat down and tried on her best frosty look, but it melted away as the waft of succulent chicken and prawns floated by her nostrils, and she looked down at the bed of golden rice and fresh green peas and felt her mouth beginning to water. She dug in her fork and savoured the taste, trying not to sigh with sheer pleasure.

Matt laughed, seeing her, and she did her best to ignore him.

After dinner, when Ben and Jade had gone to do more work on their house, Matt opened the French doors by the dining area to let in the warm evening breeze, and Lucy decided this would be a good time to phone her parents. Matt poured her a glass of chilled Chardonnay, and she took it with her over to the telephone seat at the far side of the kitchen.

'Thanks,' she said, raising her glass to him.

She chatted with her mother for a while, asking how things were at home and telling her about the babies that tore her heart to shreds in the Neonatal unit. Some time later her father came to the phone, and she told him about the property she'd gone to see the day before.

'It was so lovely,' she said, a hint of excitement in her voice. 'It's right on the waterfront, raised up so there's no danger of flooding, and there's a good bit of land all around so that the gardens can be properly landscaped. There's an old conservatory that's falling down, so that needs to be rebuilt. And, of course, there's quite a bit of work to be done inside, because it's fallen into disrepair. The dividing wall between the kitchen and utility room could be knocked down to make things bigger, but Matt agrees with me that it can all be made to look wonderful. It'll be a fantastic house when it's finished.'

'Matt was with you?'

She could feel the frown in her father's voice. 'Yes, we went to see it together. He actually made some very good points about how it can be renovated.'

'Just how much time are you and he spending together outside the house?' There was an edge of suspicion in his voice.

'Well, quite a lot, actually, since we're working together.' She batted the comment back with a tinge of humour. What did he expect, after they'd been living under the same roof all this time?

'I don't see anything amusing about this conversation,' her father said, grumpily. 'I have your welfare at heart, and I don't want any funny business going on over there. I'm responsible for the people you share a home with, and it wouldn't be right if he was to turn your head.' He warmed to his theme. 'There's too much hanky-panky going on these days, with babies born out of wedlock and couples setting up home together without bothering to tie the knot. You know how I feel about these things.'

She rolled her eyes. This was a conversation they'd had many times. 'Yes, I do…but you have to remember that I'm over twenty-one and quite old enough to do as I please.'

'As if you didn't always.' He sucked in a quick breath, priming himself for the attack.

Lucy cut in before he could get started. 'Anyway,' she said, 'about this house…I think it's a perfect development opportunity.'

'Hmm.' He thought about it for a second or two. 'I'll bid for it, then, and if it goes through, you could take charge of ordering what's needed since you're familiar with the place.'

She pulled air into her lungs. 'That would be an awful lot of work. I'd have to measure up in all the rooms, find suppliers, try and juggle costs so that we don't go over budget.'

'I'm sure you'll be fine.'

She frowned. How on earth could she take it all on? She had no idea how Jade was managing to pull everything in, but at least she had Ben to help her, and their house was a project close to their hearts.

It was the worst possible time for her to take on anything more. And yet it was something she'd dearly love to do. She'd fallen in love with that house the instant she'd seen it. Perhaps it wouldn't be so difficult, though…after all, she wouldn't need to get started straightaway because it would take quite a while for the building work to be completed, wouldn't it?

'I'll get Matt's father on to the building side of things,' her father added. 'It shouldn't take too long…a few days at most.'

She frowned. 'Matt's father isn't well, you know. Perhaps you should ease off with the work you're putting on him for a while. Everything doesn't have to be done right away, does it?'

'Time's money. How do you think we've managed to become one of the major development companies hereabouts? Certainly not through sitting still and letting the grass grow around us.'

'Even so, you've taken on a lot of extra work lately, and Matt's father might not be able to cope with it all just now. Perhaps you should bear that in mind.'

'I'm sure he'll be fine. He'd say if it was too much for him. And if he lays off the cheeses and fine wines that he likes so much, he might do better, cholesterol-wise. That's probably what's at the root of his problems,' her father said curtly.

They cut the call a short time later, and Lucy gazed around the kitchen for a moment, trying to muster enough enthusiasm to go back to her room and do some more work. Matt turned around to glance at her from the patio doors where he'd been standing, looking out over the garden.

'Why don't you come out onto the terrace for a while and get some fresh air?' he suggested. 'You've been cooped up all day, and you look as though you could do with a break.'

She didn't need much encouragement. Outside, the sun was setting, but the air was warm and it was still light. She sat in one of the white wrought-iron chairs by the table and smiled her thanks as Matt filled her glass with more wine.

'This is perfect,' she murmured. 'Just what I

need after that lovely food.' She glanced around
the garden, pleased with the lush green lawn and
colourful flower-beds that were filled with exuberant phlox and showy godetias. A delicate fragrance filled the air, and she looked over to the
fence that was covered with sweet peas in pale
shades of pink and lavender.

She sipped her wine, thankful for a few moments of peace snatched from the frantic pace
of the day.

Matt put his own glass down on the table and
came to sit in the chair beside her. 'It's been a
rough day, one way and another, with William
being in a bad way and then the baby. We could
both do with some time out.' He gave her a sideways glance and hesitated a moment before saying, 'Is everything all right with you and your
father? I couldn't help hearing some of your conversation. It sounded as though he was putting
more work on to you.'

'He's full of energy and determination, and
he imagines everyone else is the same. It's hard
to keep up with him sometimes. It's one thing

to plan an orderly approach to jobs, but when they're landed on you out of the blue it can be unsettling.'

'Can't you explain that to him?'

She smiled. 'I've tried. He doesn't see it that way, I'm afraid.'

'Why do you always do as he says? Why can't you say no to him?' Matt asked.

She shrugged. 'Actually, I don't really mind project-managing the development we looked at yesterday. In fact, I'm quite pleased at the oppor-tunity. I just wish it was my property, but, fail-ing that, I'd like to do it up as if it was my dream house...as long as I can take as long as I need and not have to rush into it while I'm in the middle of doing exams. Even Jade will take time out and leave things to Ben while those are going on.'

He nodded. 'I see all that, but the fact is you're always falling in with his plans, aren't you? No matter how much it puts you out, you always do as he asks in the end. Why is that?'

She drank some more wine and thought about it. 'I...I think probably I'm trying to win his approval. I feel as though I'm a disappointment to him.' She made a wry face. 'Well, I know that's true, in some ways.'

Matt studied her, his glance wandering over her troubled features. 'How could that be so? You must be a model daughter, I should think. You make sure everything runs smoothly in this house, that the bills are paid, the garden's in order, you've chosen a rewarding career and you're working hard at succeeding in it. What could he possibly find wrong?'

'I'm not male,' she said flatly. 'I'm not his son.' She put her glass down on the table and pulled in a shuddery breath. 'He wanted a son to follow on in the family business, to take an interest in his life's work, and his father's before him. Failing that, he hoped I would join the company, and when I chose medicine instead, he felt terribly let down. He couldn't hide it. It didn't matter that I chose a worthy career. I'd turned my back on him, as he saw it.'

'So now you do everything you can to please him.' He shook his head. 'You can't go on like that, Lucy. Something's got to give, one way or another.' He frowned. 'So what will you do? Give up on your studies and hope for the best?'

'No way.' Her brows rose in astonishment at the suggestion. Then she sobered and said with conviction, 'I have to do well—at least if I pass my exams with flying colours, he might be proud of me and then it won't matter to him so much that I chose medicine, instead. If I fail it will just give him another reason to feel that I've let him down.' Her teeth worried at her lower lip and she frowned, hardly bearing to think how it would be if that were to happen.

Matt pulled his chair closer to hers, leaning towards her and wrapping his arms around her. 'I can't get over the fact that you're under so much pressure. How do you stand it? I wish I could take some of the load from you.'

She looked up at him, touched by his obvious concern. 'You did, when you came with me to look at the house. It made everything seem so much better, somehow, because I wasn't doing it on my own. I don't know why that should be, but it helped.'

It felt good, having his arms around her. Even if it was nothing more than a friendly gesture, it was warm and comforting to snuggle up to him this way, in his arms. She could feel the heat coming from his skin, feel the steady beat of his heart next to her own, and she only had to move her head slightly for her cheek to come into contact with his throat and the strong line of his jaw. She was fascinated by his jawline, well-defined, angular, an absolutely perfect example of rugged masculinity. Being this close to him, it would be so easy to gently discover the texture of his skin with the faintest brush of her lips.

'It's probably always better to share things when you can. I'm glad I was of some help to you.'

She closed her eyes and thought about it some more. She was very relaxed, totally at ease, and that was so unusual. Where was it coming from, this sudden longing, this aching desire to press herself against him and feel his bare skin beneath her lips? Had the wine gone to her head? Perhaps it was the dazzling rays of the setting sun that were burning into her, giving her heatstroke or something, and bombarding her with all manner of strange and unaccustomed sensations.

He turned his head towards hers and their lips softly collided, his lips brushing hers with the gentlest touch, a soft caress that was so light, so delicate that for a moment she had to wonder whether it had really happened. Then her lips began to tingle, aching with unbidden desire, and suddenly there was nothing she wanted more than to feel the pressure of his mouth on hers, to have him tenderly nuzzle the small hollow beneath her jaw and taste the smooth creaminess of her skin.

'You taste of fruit and sunshine,' he murmured, kissing her softly then bringing his lips downwards to drift slowly down along the column of her throat.

She gave a tremulous sigh, wanting this to go on and on, and yet…something in her was holding back, and perhaps it was the thought of what had happened to her before that made her feel so guarded, so cautious about simply taking pleasure in the moment.

A dull thud brought them both suddenly, sharply, to their senses.

Then there was a scrabbling sound at the fence, and a small voice said inquisitively, 'What are you doing?'

'Uh…um…' Lucy straightened up in her seat and tried desperately to organise her thoughts. She knew that voice. Where was it coming from?

Matt straightened, moved abruptly away from her and appeared to shake himself slightly, as though he'd been away somewhere and now he was trying to reorientate himself.

'Can I have my ball back?' The voice came from the region of the fence, alongside the pebble patch, and as Lucy pulled herself together she realised that she could see a child's head peering through a hole low down in the fence.

'I thought we'd repaired that gap in the wood,' she said.

'Obviously not well enough to keep a three-year-old at bay,' Matt answered, his tone dry.

He stood up and walked across the grass, swooping down to retrieve a white football.

'Is this what you're looking for?' he asked, showing it to the boy.

Jacob nodded. 'I had it for my birthday. I had jelly and cake, as well, and ice cream and chocolate biscuits. My cat tipped the bowl of cream over, and he licked it all up, and then he was sick all over the kitchen floor. Mum said it served him right, 'cos he'd been pinching the tuna sandwiches when no one was looking.'

'Oh, dear.' Matt was smiling as he dropped the ball over the fence. 'Sounds as though your cat is trouble and a half.'

Jacob looked puzzled, not quite understanding what Matt was saying, but then he must have decided it didn't matter anyway because he eased his head back out of the hole, saying, 'Gotta go. Thanks for giving the ball back.'

Matt watched him over the fence for a while,

and then turned back to Lucy. 'He's a livewire, that one.'

She nodded, shading her eyes from the last embers of the sun as she looked at him. It was just as well that he'd gone over to the fence to speak to the boy for a while. It had given her time to get herself together. It had been madness, kissing Matt that way. They had to go on working together, sharing this house and trying to keep a semblance of normality, and how could they do that when sparks flared at a simple touch?

She had to stop it now, stop that mistake from escalating into something more.

'I...um...I think I'll go up to my room and do some work.' She paused, gathering her thoughts. 'What happened just now...I...uh...it...'

'I know,' he said, returning her gaze. His eyes were dark now, his expression unfathomable. 'It shouldn't have happened. Let's blame it on the wine and the end of a hard day, shall we?'

She nodded, and hurried to make her escape. Perhaps he felt as awkward about it as she did. Somehow the thought didn't exactly please her.

CHAPTER FIVE

'WHATEVER website you've accessed, it must make for very interesting reading,' Matt remarked. 'You've been engrossed in it for the last few minutes. I've been talking to you, and you've heard nothing of what I've said.'

Lucy gave a small start. She was standing at the nurses' station on the children's ward, studying the computer monitor, but now she stopped what she was doing and looked up and said, 'Sorry, what did you say?'

He was standing a little to one side of her, and she turned around to face him properly, just as he moved forward. Their bodies made a soft collision, his long, hard frame gently pressuring the softness of her curves and causing ripples of sensation to catch her unawares, surging through her from head to toe. She sucked in a deep, shaky breath. 'Did you need me for something?'

'Oh, yes,' he said huskily, a hint of humour threading his voice. His hand came to rest on the rounded swell of her hip, as though to steady her. 'All the time.' There was an unusual stillness about him, and it seemed as though he was struggling to keep himself in check. Perhaps their inadvertent, stunning contact had disturbed him every bit as much as it had shaken her.

She sent him a bemused stare. Was it possible that she could have such a profound effect on him? 'I'm not sure what…I was…' She floundered, completely at a loss. 'I was looking something up,' she tried to explain. For the life of her, she couldn't think straight. Her whole body was hot from that sizzling contact, and even when he moved back a pace, the heat stayed with her, fire coursing through her veins.

'Mmm…I gathered that,' he said in a roughened voice. He cleared his throat and made an effort to pull himself together. 'It was nothing important. I was asking if you wanted to try one of these chocolate éclairs. I picked them up from the bakery at lunchtime.'

He held out a box to her and she looked down at the delectable choux pastries it contained, with their coating of sensuously smooth, dark chocolate.

'Oh, I see…' She struggled to get back on an even keel. 'Um…they look great, don't they?' She gazed at them wistfully for a moment and then said on a sorrowful note, 'But I don't think I could eat a thing right now. I'm far too much on edge. Professor Farnham's expecting me to examine one of his patients and make a diagnosis, and I'm a bit anxious about it. On the face of it, it should be simple, but it always makes me nervous, being put on the spot. And you can never tell with these things. There may be something I'm missing.'

'It's okay. Maybe later, then, when you're not so wound up. I'll ask Mandy if she'll put them in the fridge for me. There are enough for all the staff.' He smiled, putting the box to one side. 'What's the case you're looking at? Perhaps I can help in some way.'

She dragged her thoughts back to the work in hand, trying to be professional about things. It wasn't easy, with Matt standing so close, near enough so that she could see the strong column of his throat and feel the warmth emanating from him.

He was waiting patiently, and she determinedly shut out those errant thoughts and said, 'She's a young girl, twelve years old. When I looked at her notes, I saw that she'd been complaining of a really bad throat and of feeling unwell. Her GP prescribed a course of antibiotics, believing there was an infection, but they don't seem to have worked. She went to see him again this afternoon and he made an urgent appointment for us to see her here.' She frowned. 'Straightaway I thought of tonsillitis, but I suspect there's something more to it, or why would she be here, instead of being treated at home? Apparently, she can hardly bear to open her mouth, and she's having trouble swallowing.'

He was thoughtful for a moment. 'Perhaps you should look for the complications of tonsillitis, such as a middle-ear infection, strep infection or even rheumatic fever. Then again, if one side of the throat is more swollen than the other, you might be dealing with an abscess.'

'Yes.' She nodded. 'I wondered about that. I'll go and have a look at her—if she can stand it.' She made a faint grimace. 'I feel really sorry for her, but at least the professor prescribed some painkillers for her in the meantime. Anyway—' her mouth curved briefly '—thanks for the advice. I just hope I get it right when I present the case to the professor...'

'I'm sure you'll be fine,' he said.

'I hope so.' All these activities and procedures were recorded in her electronic profile and became part of the assessment that would eventually prove her fitness to practise as a doctor. She couldn't afford to make any mistakes.

Matt went with her a few minutes later to the treatment room where the girl was waiting, along with her mother. Professor Farnham was already there, talking to them.

Lucy acknowledged the professor with a smile and a nod, and then explained to the mother and daughter that she was a medical student. She introduced Matt to them, and said, 'Dr Berenger will be looking after you, Melanie, but with your permission I'd like to take a look at your throat.'

The girl agreed, and Lucy said quietly, 'It's very red and inflamed—I can see how painful it must be for you.' To the professor, she added, 'There are no white spots on there, and her throat is closing up so the channel is quite narrow.'

She handed her slim-line torch to Matt, and he took a quick look at the girl's throat, shining the light into her mouth so that he could see her tonsils.

When he had finished, Lucy glanced at her patient and said, 'Thanks, Melanie. You can relax now for a bit. It's uncomfortable for you, I know, but I'm sure we'll get you sorted out very shortly. Just sit back and rest, and let the painkillers do their job. I'll leave you for just a moment or two while I go and have a word with the professor.'

The girl nodded, clearly unwilling to speak because of her discomfort. Her mother sat in a chair beside the treatment couch, and the two of them tried to distract themselves for a while by watching the TV screen that was suspended on the far wall.

Lucy pulled in a deep breath and outlined her findings to her boss. 'She's been unwell for a while, with a sore throat that has become steadily worse. It's very inflamed, more swollen on one side than the other. I can't see any pus escaping at the moment, but even so I believe it's a peri-tonsillar abscess, otherwise known as quinsy.'

He nodded. 'And what should we do about it?'

'Needle aspiration and intravenous antibiotics.'

'Anything else?'

Lucy's mind went blank for a second or two. Had she forgotten something? A wave of panic hit her, and a rush of heat flowed through her body, bringing small beads of perspiration to her brow. Then she blinked and said on a questioning note, 'We should admit her for an overnight stay, or possibly longer, until we see that the antibiotics are beginning to work?'

'That's it. Good.' Lucy felt an enormous sense of relief and her shoulders relaxed a little. She hadn't quite realised how tense she'd been until then.

The professor smiled and then glanced at Matt, who was standing beside him. 'Perhaps you could see to all that, with Lucy's help?'

'I will.'

The professor left them, and Matt smiled at Lucy. 'See? That wasn't so bad, was it?'

'No, it wasn't. I don't know why I let these things worry me so much.' Calmer now, she helped Matt to set up a trolley with needles and suction equipment.

'The doctor will give you an anaesthetic,' she explained to Melanie, 'so you won't feel any pain when he draws the fluid from the abscess. It shouldn't take more than a few minutes, and then we'll set up an intravenous line in your arm so that we can give you strong antibiotics to clear up any remaining infection.'

She and Matt worked together to drain the abscess. He chatted to the girl and her mother as he carried out the procedure, putting his patient at ease, and Lucy marvelled at how gentle he was. He'd said once that he was torn between specialising in A and E or Paediatrics, but after seeing him at work over these last few weeks she was sure he would make a great children's doctor.

Some half an hour later, after they had cleared up and left Mandy to make arrangements for the girl to be admitted, they went over to the staff lounge to take a break.

'Perhaps, now that's over, you'll feel more like eating your éclair,' Matt commented, fetching the cakes from the fridge and sliding the box across the worktop to her. 'I told you everything would be okay. Professor Farnham's a good man. He's on your side—he wants you to succeed.'

'I know. And it was a really simple case. It's just that you're under scrutiny in these situations, and when someone's watching me, everything flies out of my head.'

'It's happened to all of us at some time. You get used to it in the end.' He handed her a plate and poured coffee into two mugs, adding cream and sugar.

Lucy bit into the chocolate éclair and gave a sigh of satisfaction. 'Mmm…mmm…mmm, that is so-o-o-o good,' she murmured, savouring the moment.

Matt smiled, giving her a curious sideways look. 'I think Jade used to wonder how you manage to keep that hourglass figure—she thought it was because you watched what you eat all the time, but that isn't true, is it? I've seen you eat fries and cream and all sorts of goodies. You're just naturally made that way, aren't you?' His glance moved over her, gliding over the soft blouse that gently caressed her curves and the skirt whose gentle folds drifted over her long, shapely legs. His gaze came to rest on the honey gold of her hair, the tousled curls held back with two clips.

Lucy paused for a moment, holding the last bit of cream cake aloft. She didn't know what to make of Matt. He'd remarked on her figure in a casual, natural kind of manner, and it was clear he liked the way she looked, but he never pushed the issue. Where other men would have followed up, Matt held back, and yet she knew he wasn't oblivious to her. He'd been shaken when they'd bumped into each other earlier, that much had been obvious. But for the rest…she didn't know what was going on inside his head. He was an enigma.

She finished off the éclair and then licked the remnants of cream from her lips with the tip of her tongue. 'That was so good. Thanks for that. It was really thoughtful of you to bring cakes in.'

He acknowledged that with a smile, but then his mobile phone began to ring, its familiar guitar melody breaking into the silence.

He looked at the display. 'It's my mother,' he said with a frown. 'I hope that doesn't mean something's happened to my father.'

Lucy moved away to give him space to take

the call, but she couldn't help hearing his comments and after the initial exchange of greetings she noted the growing concern in his voice.

'There's no point in getting yourself worked up about it, Mum,' he said. 'Dad's a grown man and he has to be clear about what he can do or can't do, and it's up to him to say if something's too much for him.' There was a pause, then, 'I know…I know…he's always been that way, trying to please everyone and never turning down work. But, as you say, there has to come a point when he must say it can't be done.'

Another pause. Lucy swallowed the rest of her coffee and hoped her father wasn't behind this latest influx of work that was causing problems for Matt's father. Deep down, though, she already knew the answer to that. It was the waterfront house that would have been the straw that had broken the camel's back—her father would have made the bid for it at auction, and what was the betting he had succeeded in getting it?

Matt finished the call, and she glanced at him, seeing the bleak downturn of his mouth.

'I hardly dare ask,' she ventured. 'It sounds as though my father managed to buy the house.'

He nodded. 'So now my dad is trying to work out how to fit it into his schedule. His men are already behind with the work on a new housing development, so this is just one more difficulty to add to the mix. My mother's getting agitated about the whole thing because he suggested delaying their summer holiday, or failing that he wanted her to go on ahead without him, and said he would join her later.' He winced. 'You can imagine her reaction to that, can't you? My mother always had a short fuse. I certainly wouldn't want to mess with her.'

'You can't really blame her, though.' Lucy wished there was something she could say or do to defuse the situation, but she'd already spoken to her father about it, and he wasn't paying her any attention. 'She's thinking about your father's health. That's her priority. She must be very worried. It must be so upsetting to see him snowed under this way.'

'Yes.' He went over to the coffee machine and

topped up his mug. 'I don't know what the answer is. I talked to my brother about it, and he said the men are working all hours to get everything done, but the pressure's on, with deadlines and penalty clauses coming into play, and both my brother and my dad tried to talk to your father about this, but he seems oblivious to any of their concerns. He's purely a businessman, looking at the end profit—he seems to think it'll all work itself out.'

She looked at him. 'I'm sorry.'

He shrugged. 'You've done nothing wrong.' He gave a wry grin. 'But you can bet the Clements name is a sore point with my mother right now. You could say she's spitting bricks.'

Lucy pulled a face. 'I'm afraid my father has that effect on some people. I suppose it's understandable if she's not too happy with us right now. Perhaps it's just as well we don't run into her all that often. It'll give her time to cool off.'

She thought back to the time when they had been teenagers and they had all lived in the same Berkshire village. She hadn't known Matt very well back then, but there had been occasions when their parents had organised get-togethers and invited the company's employees over to one or the other's house. Both she and Matt had lived in big country houses, where there had been ample room for these kinds of social functions, and quite often the party had spilled out into the grounds of the estate.

'Do you remember when we used to have those company parties?' she said now. 'We used to alternate, didn't we, with your father hosting the do one year, and the next it would be my father's turn.' She smiled. 'I used to feel really self-conscious at those affairs. One year, especially, when I was about seventeen, I found myself surrounded by a lot of people who were at least ten years older than me, and most of them were talking business. I tried to take an interest and ask all the right questions, but after an hour or two I'd had enough.'

'I remember.' His eyes darkened as he thought back to those days. 'You slipped outside. I saw my brother going after you into the garden, and neither of you reappeared for quite some time.'

She laughed. 'Kyle showed me all the hiding places on your land. We dodged from the summerhouse to the gazebo and even the back of the garden shed, when we saw my father on the prowl, looking for me.'

His gaze flickered. 'I don't suppose he ever caught up with you. Kyle was too canny for that. Back then, he had a huge crush on you. He'd have done anything to keep you with him for as long as possible.'

'We were so young, without a care in the world.' She looked at him curiously. 'What happened to you? I don't remember you coming out to join us.'

His mouth made a wry twist. 'Kyle was my older brother. He gave me strict instructions to stay out of the way. You were the girl every guy wanted, and those parties were the perfect opportunity for him to cosy up to you, especially the one when you were sweet seventeen.' He frowned. 'I told him he'd better treat you right. You were young and innocent and I was concerned for you. Kyle's changed now, he's decent and straightforward, but back then he was very casual in the way he treated girls. So I wasn't going to make it easy for him. I guessed what was going on in his mind, so I hid all the keys to the outbuildings.'

Lucy's eyes widened. 'You did?' She chuckled. 'I wondered about that. Kyle was so put out when we couldn't get inside any of them.' Why had Matt done it? Was it just, as he'd seemed to imply, that he had been protective, or could it be that he'd had some feelings for her back then?

She shook off the thought. He'd never said anything, either at the time or since. Even so, she couldn't resist saying lightly, 'Perhaps there was a bit of brotherly rivalry going on there?'

'I don't know. I didn't think about it too deeply. I suppose I just acted on instinct.'

Her expression sobered. 'Anyway, perhaps it was for the best. My father was always very uptight about any boys who came near me.'

'I don't think he's changed much on that score.'

'No, you're probably right about that.' She

frowned, looking at him oddly. How would he know that? But perhaps he'd caught the gist of telephone conversations she'd had with her father. Her father was ultra-protective of her, and he was always going to try to vet the men in her life, even when she had grown up and was living away from home.

She brushed those thoughts aside and said, 'So if my father's bought the waterfront house, it means he'll be asking me to project-manage the renovations before too long. I ought to go back there sometime soon and take another look and see exactly what needs to be done, just in case your father decides to send someone down there to make a start.' She thought about it some more, trying to work out when she could spare the time. 'Perhaps I'd better go after work today. I'm pretty sure the agent will still have a key so that we can get in. I daren't leave it any longer, because I have my practical exams coming up in a few days' time.'

'You could do without the extra work right

now,' Matt pointed out. 'Can't you leave it until the exams are over and done with?'

'I could…but then the workmen will follow the rough draft I gave my father, and they'll add their own interpretation to some of the alterations. I'd sooner they had more detailed instructions—it's my very own project, and I can see it in my mind's eye. I'd hate it not to turn out as I wanted it.'

'What about the revision time you're missing out on? I thought that was important to you, as well?'

'It is, but I can make up for it tomorrow when I have a study session.'

He nodded. 'It sounds as though you have it all worked out. I'll go with you, if you like. You'll need someone to hold the other end of the tape and hoist that creaky loft ladder down so that you can take a look at the attic rooms.' He reflected on that for a while. 'Perhaps your first priority should be to get a proper staircase put in.'

'Yes, you're right. Thanks, Matt. I'd appreciate it if you came along.' She sent him a grateful look and then went to wash her coffee mug at the sink. 'You seem to have a vision for what needs doing.'

The door to the lounge opened then, and Mandy dipped her head into the room. 'We've a seriously ill child coming in,' she said, 'a little boy who was knocked down by a car. He's five years old, with injuries to his head, chest and leg. He's being transferred to us from A and E. He should be in Intensive Care by rights, but they can't take any more patients in there at the moment. Professor Farnham says we can manage him here, instead. I'm going to be with him on a one-to-one basis, and the professor wants you to oversee things when the registrar's not available, Matt.'

'Okay, we're on it.' Matt was already striding towards the door.

Lucy hurried after him, anxious to be part of the team caring for this desperately ill child. A head injury was always serious, with the risk of swelling to the brain and consequent dangerous outcomes.

When she reached the ward, she found that the

child's mother was in tears, and the father was white-faced and shaken. 'He ran into the road,' he said. 'I tried to stop him but he pulled away from me to go after a kitten. The driver tried to stop, he slammed his brakes on…but it was too late. Tom was right in his path.'

Lucy did her best to soothe them, but it was hard. She could only imagine the stress they were under. Wouldn't she feel exactly the same if it was her child lying there, unconscious, not moving, not speaking?

'Dr Berenger will make sure that he's well looked after,' she told them. 'Tom's in good hands.' She took them into the office and made a fresh pot of tea, talking to them and answering their questions as best she could while Mandy and Matt checked the boy over and assessed what needed to be done.

'He'll be staying in a side ward,' she said, 'right next to the nurses' station, but one of the nurses will be assigned to watch over him the whole time.' It was difficult for her to know what to say without knowing the particulars of the boy's condition, but the parents told her that their son's right leg had been broken in the accident, and he had been to Theatre to have the fracture fixed and the leg set in a cast.

'I think the doctors were most worried about his head injury, though,' the boy's mother said, her eyes filling with tears all over again. 'He was tossed up in the air and landed first on his leg and then his head came down on the road. I couldn't believe what was happening.' Her voice broke, and her husband laid a comforting arm around her shoulders.

There was a knock on the door, and a nurse said quietly, 'The boy's grandparents are here, a Mr and Mrs Cavendish. Perhaps you'd all be better off in the waiting room. There's more room in there.' She looked apologetic at having to move them on, but Lucy stood up and prepared to show them the way.

The boy's father stiffened at hearing the news. 'They're going to blame me, aren't they? They're going to want to know why I didn't hold on to him more tightly.'

The young woman winced. 'More likely, they'll want to know why they weren't told right away about the accident. All I could think about was Tom. I left everything else to you.'

'I was in shock,' he answered. 'I couldn't think straight. I just knew I had to call an ambulance. The rest of it's a blur.'

Lucy sensed trouble ahead, but she said nothing, leading them instead to the waiting room and standing by as they greeted the woman's parents. 'I'll leave you to talk for a while,' she murmured, conscious of the sombre, tense atmosphere that pervaded the room. 'If you want refreshments, there's a drinks machine in the corridor, and you'll find a cafeteria on the ground floor. Someone will come along in a while and let you know how Tom's doing.'

They weren't paying her much attention. The grandparents' expressions were fraught, while the boy's father was remote, caught up in his own inner battle with guilt and grief.

'How's he doing?' she asked when she reached the side ward. Matt was writing out a medication chart while Mandy set up a drip and checked the infusion meter.

'He's stable for the moment,' Matt answered. 'The chest injury's not serious—it's the head and leg injury we have to worry about.' He handed her the boy's file. 'You might want to read up on this and check the CT scan and X-rays on the computer. The professor will probably quiz you on what's going on.'

'Thanks.' She took the file he offered, but instead of reading it straight away she spent some time looking at the small boy who lay motionless on the bed. It broke her up inside to see a child hurt this way. How could she even think of making Paediatrics her specialty when she couldn't bear to see the awful things that happened to the children in her care?

'We've done all we can for him for now, anyway,' Matt said. 'We'll keep a lookout for any rise in pressure within the brain, and keep our fingers crossed that he remains stable.'

He checked his watch. 'We should have been off duty about half an hour ago, and we should leave now if you want to go over to the house. I'll hand over to James, and then we'll head straight off to the Thames, if you like—or did you want to go home first to get something to eat? I don't suppose a cake is enough to sustain either of us for long, is it?'

'I'd sooner go straight there,' Lucy said, 'if you don't mind. I like to get the work out of the way first, and then I can relax. I know it's my turn to cook tonight, but Ben and Jade won't be there—they're driving over to Jade's parents' home to talk about their wedding plans. It won't be too long for them now...they set the date for straight after the exams are finished.' She shook her head. 'I don't know how Jade manages to fit everything in, though at least she's given up working part time at the café, which is one less thing for her to worry about.'

'I don't think she had any intention of giving it up,' Matt said with a crooked grin. 'It was more that Ben was very persuasive. He said that they were going to be married very soon, and he wanted her to be able to spend more time with him. He told her he'd take care of things so she didn't need to worry.'

Lucy nodded. 'She looks happy, anyway. I expect her mother's helped a good deal by sorting out a lot of the wedding preparations. She was the one who arranged for me to have a fitting for the bridesmaid's dress.'

He smiled. 'I keep forgetting it's going to happen within the next few weeks. I guess it'll be quite an occasion.' He frowned. 'We'll have to think about getting them a wedding present. How do you feel about you and I going into the city to hunt something out? I'd sooner have your input on this.'

'Sounds good to me.' She looked thoughtful. 'I suppose we'd better get on to it fairly soon.'

'Next weekend, then?'

'That's fine by me, but I've no idea what we should get for them.' She screwed up her face, thinking about it.

Matt gave a light shrug. 'Perhaps we'll just generally look around and see what strikes us.'

'Yes. I'm sure between us we'll come up with

something.' She left him then, going off to make a quick, final check of all her patients while Matt dealt with the handover to the registrar.

Over in Neonatal, baby Sarah was still on the ventilator, still unable to breathe on her own, while here on the children's ward young William was weak and suffering from low blood pressure, which had a tendency to make him feel dizzy and faint. The trauma of the accident, followed by surgery for a damaged spleen, had taken all his strength away. He didn't have the energy to respond to her light-hearted chat, so she gave his hand an encouraging, gentle squeeze.

'You'll be all right,' she told him. 'Just keep getting plenty of rest.' All she could hope for was that both of them would keep on fighting their way back to health.

'All set?' Matt came to find her as she was once more gazing unhappily down at the small boy with the head injury who had just been admitted to the side ward. Life wasn't fair. It shouldn't be this way. She willed him to recover.

'Yes, I'm ready.'

The journey took about half an hour on the train, and at the end of it Lucy was glad to emerge from the station into the late-afternoon sunshine. The island, with its lush green trees and the wild flowers that grew along the river bank, was as inviting as ever. Lucy felt her spirits lift.

They spent a couple of hours looking around the house, trying to decide where a wall should be displaced here or the plumbing should be altered there, and Lucy took care to write everything down in a notebook.

'There's an awful lot of work to be done,' she said, gazing around when they had finally decided to call it a day.

'But it will be well worth it. It'll be beautiful when it's finished, and your father should get a good price for it. These houses don't come on the market very often, and people will scramble to be in the queue to buy it.'

'Yes, I suppose you're right.' She sighed. 'It's way more than I could ever afford.'

'Are you looking to buy your own place? I

thought you were well set up in your father's house.'

'You're right. I'm lucky, I know it, and I should be grateful that I don't have the trouble others have, finding somewhere to live. It's just that I sometimes long to have a place of my own, somewhere that's truly mine. It's silly of me, really, to be even thinking of it, I suppose. That's way ahead in the future.' She frowned, looking around. 'There's something about this place, though. Even as it is, in its rundown state, I feel peaceful here, as though it's a kind of sanctuary where I can leave all my troubles behind.'

He sent her a quizzical glance. 'I can see your point, but you've set your hopes up a bit high, haven't you? It's a shame, because that way you could end up being disappointed.'

'I know.'

He laid a hand around her waist, and somehow the intimate touch was warmly comforting. 'Shall we go and see what the pub down the road is like? I'll buy you dinner. I saw that they do meals when we passed by the other day.

Maybe that will help to cheer you up. I get the feeling that this has been a difficult day for you, one way and another.'

'Thanks.' She smiled at him. 'I'd like that.'

The pub was a rambling old building, painted white and set back a little from the riverside. There was a wide footpath alongside the water and a paved area where bench tables had been set out so that people could drink or eat out there on a summer's day.

The evening was still warm, with only a faint breeze to disturb the reeds at the water's edge, and for a while they stood and watched the boats go by and followed the meanderings of a pair of mallard ducks and their offspring, exploring the foliage.

'Do you want to eat out here?' Matt asked, looking around. 'We could sit at one of the tables by the tree over there, if you like.' He pointed to a spot where the sun's rays dappled the leaves of an old beech tree. Nearby, a young couple relaxed with their baby and the family dog, which had stretched out on the towpath, every now and again lifting his head to sniff the air.

'Yes, that's fine.' They went over there and sat down, studying the menus that had been left on the slats of the wooden table. 'Oh, this looks great,' Lucy said. 'I wonder if the food's as good as they make it sound—sun-dried tomatoes, aromatic roasted vegetables and caramelised red-onion chutney—and it all looks so colourful. I didn't realise I was so hungry until I sat down here.'

'Me, too.' He grinned. 'You tend to forget about food when you're busy on the wards. And if things are hectic, it can be several hours before you get to eat again.' He studied the menu, and after a while he stood up and went to place their order.

Lucy gazed at the gently flowing river, watching the damselflies dip and dart over its surface. At the water's edge there were clusters of creamy white meadowsweet, and here and there graceful purple willow herb swayed gently in the evening air.

'This is a crisp and fruity white wine, chilled to perfection, or so I'm told,' Matt said with a smile, placing a wine glass on the table in front of her. He was drinking lager, served in a tall, thin glass that had frosted over, with small rivulets of condensation running down the side.

'Cheers,' she said, raising her glass to him, and he answered, clinking his glass to hers.

'Good times,' he murmured.

'Yes, we could do with some of those.'

The waitress brought their meals—steak, topped with cheddar and grilled bacon for Matt, and chicken-and-bacon salad for Lucy.

'This looks wonderful,' she said. 'I'm glad we decided to come here.'

'I guess we could both do with a break.' He glanced at her. 'I could see you were troubled today, looking in on the children who were so poorly. The fact is we work in a difficult profession. Most people don't ever, in a lifetime, have to deal with the things we come across every day.'

'No, that's true. It's upsetting to see babies on ventilators, fighting for their lives, and as if that isn't bad enough, we see young children coming in with nasty injuries and we have to do our best to patch them up.'

He speared a button mushroom with his fork and then hesitated, studying her expression. 'You didn't seem to have too much of a problem with young William, but when I saw you looking at the small boy who came in today—Tom—you seemed to be more disturbed by his condition than usual. Are you worried about his prospects of recovery?'

'I suppose there's something of that.' She sipped her wine. 'It made me think about why I decided to take up medicine as a career.'

'Are you beginning to have doubts?'

'Yes, I think I am. Now that I'm actually working in a hospital, on the wards, I'm not sure whether I'm cut out for it...for that kind of emergency or the specialist type of medicine.'

She thought he might be shocked or disturbed by what she'd said, but he studied her thoughtfully and asked, 'So what was it that made you want to go to medical school in the first place?

Was it just a vague idea about wanting to help people, to make them well again?'

'No, not really.' She sliced off a piece of new potato and swirled it in the mayonnaise at the side of her plate. 'When I was young, around twelve or thirteen, I saw a neighbour's child knocked down by a car. I was with a friend at the time and, of course, we were both horrified by what we saw. The paramedics came and worked with an emergency doctor, getting her onto a spinal board, putting a tube down her throat to help her breathe, starting up an intravenous line. Of course, I didn't understand much of what they were doing back then, but I knew that they saved her life. She would have bled to death on the road if they hadn't acted quickly.'

She paused, thinking back to that time. 'It made me realise what a worthwhile career medicine was, and I wanted to be able to save lives the way those men did that day.' She'd been so impressed by the way the medics had handled the situation, and later, when she'd gone to visit the girl in hospital, she was amazed at her recovery.

'And now you've seen it from the professional side of things, it worries you?'

'It does a bit. Not that I couldn't do what needs to be done to save a life, but that working with children, working on the emergency side of things, isn't what I want to deal with every day. Does that sound odd to you?' She gave him a worried look. 'I gave up the chance to work with my father when it was what he wanted most of all, and I still don't want to do that, but I'm having doubts about what would be best thing for me to do.' She frowned. 'I'm not explaining myself very well, am I?'

'I think I understand. It doesn't sound odd to me at all. A lot of people have doubts…after all, it's a big step you're taking.' He finished the last of his steak, and swallowed some of his lager. She watched his throat move, and her glance went to his strong forearms, the sleeves of his shirt rolled back, exposing a gold watch on his wrist.

'But I do think you need to have a bit more confidence in yourself,' he went on. 'I haven't seen you put a foot wrong, and I know that one day you'll make a terrific doctor...maybe not a hospital doctor, if that troubles you, but you're certainly cut out for a medical career.' He smiled reassuringly at her. 'Perhaps you might want to work as a GP one day. I think you would probably enjoy working with children at some point. I saw how you were with baby Sarah, and again with William before he went for surgery—you were gentle and involved, and it occurred to me that maybe a mother-and-baby clinic would be more your style, as part of general practice.'

'Oh...' She looked startled, and then, after a second or two, as his words sank in she gave him a dazzling smile. 'I hadn't looked at it that way. I felt like a failure because I was worried about my reactions to these very sick children—but I think you could be right. I can see myself working in a GP's surgery one day. Thank you for that.'

He grinned crookedly. 'Glad to be of service, ma'am. Maybe we should drink to that.' He lifted his glass once more. 'To fulfilling your dreams, whatever they might be.' He looked into her eyes, and as they toasted one another with their drinks it was as though a warm, intimate bond was forged between them.

They chatted over caramelised apple pie, for Lucy, and strawberry cheesecake, for Matt, and then finished off the meal with liqueur coffees.

'That was absolutely perfect—heavenly,' Lucy said on a sigh, as they left the pub sometime later and began walking back along the towpath. 'Thank you.'

Matt started to say something, but his phone rang at that moment and he stopped walking and gave her an apologetic smile as he started to answer it. She waited, wondering who was calling him, then watched as the colour slowly drained from his face.

'What's wrong?' she asked as he slid the phone back into his pocket. 'Has something bad happened?'

'My father's had a heart attack,' he said, in a strained voice. 'I must go and see him.'

'Oh, Matt, I'm so sorry.' She put her arms around him, hugging him. 'Is there anything I can do? Would you like me to go with you?'

He looked distracted. 'No. I'll go alone, thank you.' He hugged her in return and then gently released himself from her embrace, his hands curving lightly around her arms. 'I'll see you home safely and then I must go. If we leave now, I can be at the hospital within the hour.'

'Of course.' She understood that he needed to be with his father right now, and it was clear that he was deeply shocked by the news. He had to go and find out just how bad things were, and he wanted to be able to comfort his mother and offer her his support. Lucy understood all that. Of course he didn't want her there with him. Even so, a tiny part of her felt as though she'd been rejected all the same.

CHAPTER SIX

'TOM, can you hear me?' Lucy gently stroked the small boy's hand. Throughout the morning she had been talking, on and off, to the five-year-old, testing his responses and trying to assess his level of consciousness.

'He's not doing so well,' she told Mandy with a frown, moving away from the bed, out of earshot of the child's mother and grandmother. 'I was getting some kind of a response earlier on, but now nothing much is registering. Perhaps we should give Matt a call.'

'Okay. I'll go and see to it,' the nurse answered, concern showing in her grey eyes. 'He said we should let him know if there was any change in his condition.'

'Thanks, Mandy. He's over in Neonatal, taking a look at baby Sarah.'

She'd been working with Matt for the first part of the morning, but he hadn't been his usual self, and that wasn't surprising, given what had happened to his father. He was distant, locked into a place within himself that she couldn't reach. Last night he'd come back to the house late, after being with his father for most of the evening. He hadn't said much to anyone, and she'd seen that he'd been very worried about his father's sudden collapse. She'd tried to offer him comfort and sympathy, but he'd been distracted, his whole manner strained and very quiet.

Mandy went to make the call, and Lucy studied the monitors by the child's bed, alarmed by the rise in his blood pressure and the slowing down of his heart rate.

'What's happening? Is something wrong?' Mrs Granger had been sitting quietly with her mother by the bedside, but now she called out in alarm as a sudden bleeping came from one of the monitors.

Tom was restless, his arms and legs twitching every now and again. He started to vomit, and Lucy hurried forward with a kidney bowl, holding it in place for him, and then afterwards, when he had finished being sick, she wiped his brow with a cool, damp cloth. She was relieved that his endotracheal tube was firmly in place, protecting his airway, so there was no danger of him choking. In her experience, it was unusual for a child to vomit once the tube was in place, but she was coming across new things every day.

'It seems that there's some swelling inside his skull,' she explained to the anxious women. 'We have to bring that down and try to make him more comfortable.'

Tom's grandmother frowned. The stress she was going through was clearly visible in her eyes, and her back was stiff with tension. 'I'll never forgive Jack for this,' she said tersely, shooting a glance at her daughter. 'He shouldn't have let the boy run ahead of him in the street—it was an accident waiting to happen.'

'He didn't do that. Jack was holding his hand,' the boy's mother answered wearily, close to tears, her voice thickening. 'Tom pulled away from him.'

'So he says. You said you were looking at something else and not paying much attention, so you only have his word for it.'

Lucy saw the distress in Miriam Granger's eyes and decided it was time to intervene. 'Ladies, Tom may be able to hear you,' she warned softly. 'Either way, the tone of your voices might be enough to upset him and make his condition worse. I think it would be best if you were to try to stay calm around him.'

'Of course,' Mrs Granger said in a guilty tone. She looked uncomfortable, glancing at her mother as though she feared she might disagree. 'I'm sorry.'

Mrs Cavendish remained quiet, pressing her lips together as though she was finding it a struggle to keep to herself all the things she wanted to say, but after a short while, when she said nothing further, Lucy breathed a silent sigh of relief.

Her satisfaction was short-lived, though. In the next moment the little boy began to shake, his body movements becoming stronger and faster paced as a seizure took hold of him. Lucy saw it happen with a growing sense of frustration. She knew what to do, but as a student she wasn't allowed to prescribe medication, and that put her in a quandary. She looked around, ready to call for help, and saw that Matt had already come into the room and was heading their way. Relief flooded through her.

'How long has this been going on?' he asked.

'It just started. I was just about to call for help.'

'That's okay.' He nodded and left the bedside, coming back within a few seconds armed with a syringe. 'I'm going to give him anti-convulsant medication to try and bring the seizure under control,' he explained to the boy's mother.

After he had given the medication, he turned to Lucy and said in a low voice, 'As soon as we have the seizure under control, I'll sedate him and give him a painkiller and then we'll try a diuretic to see if we can reduce some of the swelling in his brain.'

'Will that be enough?' She was worried about

this little boy. He looked so vulnerable, lying there, and she wished there was more she could do to help him.

'Possibly not. We'll have to consult with the neurologist—it could be that we'll need to drain off some of the cerebrospinal fluid to ease the pressure on his brain.' He checked the catheter that was already in place in the boy's head, ready for this event, and then waited for the seizure to come to an end.

He noted Tom's vital signs and prepared the sedative and diuretic. 'That's good...it looks as though he's coming out of it...the convulsion's stopped,' he murmured after a while. 'Let's raise the head of the bed slightly and try to ease some of that pressure.'

Lucy helped him, and together they looked after the child for the next few minutes, checking the monitors constantly. Lucy was aware that treating a brain-injured child was always going to be a delicate balance—they had to weigh one drug against another, because any one of them might cause unwanted side effects that could hinder recovery. Sedation might cause the child's blood pressure to drop even more, but seizures and restlessness placed more demands on him and could cause pressure to rise dangerously within the brain.

Matt was calm throughout this time, and Lucy marvelled at how capable and efficient he was as he checked tubes and drips, adjusted the medication dosage and found time to speak to the child's mother and grandmother. When the neurologist arrived on the ward, he explained what was going on and discussed with him what needed to be done next.

'Keep him under strict observation, Mandy,' he said now. 'Note everything down on his chart at fifteen-minute intervals and call me if there's any sign of his condition deteriorating. I'll finish off the ward round and then, if I'm needed, I'll be in the cardiac-care unit with my father.'

'Okay. I'll take good care of him,' Mandy answered. 'I hope your father's a bit better today when you go and look in on him.'

'So do I.' Matt's expression was grim, and Lucy's heart went out to him.

'Have you been to see him yet this morning?' she asked, as she followed him to the next bay.

He shook his head. 'I was on duty too early, so I haven't had a chance yet, but I phoned for an update. It's not looking good…but I suppose these are still early days. The scans showed a huge clot in one of his arteries. My mother's in pieces.'

She touched his arm lightly, wanting to be close to him. 'It must be really difficult for you, having to come into work when you're so worried. I don't know how you're able to cope. I don't think I'd be able to concentrate if something like that happened to one of my parents.'

He exhaled deeply. 'I don't have much choice but to carry on. We're short-handed here, and Administration has been finding it difficult to bring in locums of late because of the holiday period.' He winced. 'Besides, I'm no good at sitting around. Last night I couldn't do anything but watch him lying there in bed, so ill, and I felt helpless, having to sit back and let others take care of him. I was able to comfort my mother, of course, but I can't be there for her twenty-four hours of the day, much as I'd like to help her.'

Lucy shot him a quick, anxious glance. 'I wasn't criticising you in any way, please don't think that...it's just that I've watched you with the children this morning, and you've been so good with them. No matter how bad you're feeling inside, you've managed to stay professional. I really admire you for that.'

He gave her a brief smile that barely touched his lips. 'You've been a great help to me, keeping me on track, alerting me when things were going on with the patients. I've been trying to do my best, but I'll admit my mind's been elsewhere.' He looked at her with a quizzical expression. 'Actually, I'm not quite sure what you're doing here today. You have your clinical examination this afternoon, don't you? I'd have expected you to be at home, swotting up or talking things through with Jade. I know she's really worried about these exams. Ben told me she hasn't been able to concentrate on anything lately, not even their wedding plans.'

'I know.' Lucy sighed. 'She wanted to shut herself in her room to revise this morning, but I was too jittery to sit still and do that, so I decided to come to the hospital instead and keep busy. I'll be meeting Jade in around an hour for lunch, and then we'll go to the exam hall together.'

He gave her a sympathetic glance. 'I'm sure you'll do just fine. Remember you get points for each step of the procedure so you'll pick up easy marks for simple things like washing your hands before and after examining the patient, and for communication skills—so make sure you introduce yourself, and explain what you are going to do. Take a deep breath before you speak, so that you come across clearly. It's as much about your examination technique and the procedures you follow as it is about finding the correct diagnosis.'

'I'll try to bear that in mind.'

'Like I said, I'm sure you'll be all right.' He gently squeezed her shoulder, his long fingers lightly kneading her taut muscles and sending warm, comforting ripples of sensation coursing through her body. 'You've had lots of practice with patients on the wards. Just imagine that each one you come across this afternoon is someone you're treating at this hospital.'

She gave him a smile. 'I'll try. Thanks for the advice, Matt, and the encouragement.' She sobered, studying his strong, angular features. 'This is all the wrong way round. I should be sympathising with you and offering you support. I know how much you care for your father, and this must have come as an awful shock to you.'

She sighed, thinking about Sam Berenger. 'I remember seeing him at home, some years back, at those parties we were talking about the other day, and he was always good to me. He showed an interest in what I was doing and he was keen to know what I wanted out of life. I wish there was something I could do to help. Maybe, one day, when he's up to it, I could perhaps go with you to see him?'

'Thanks. I know you want to help...' His voice

took on a cautious note. 'I know you and my dad got on really well together, but let's just see how things go for a while, shall we? He's definitely not up to seeing anyone outside the family just yet.'

Lucy frowned. Perhaps she'd imagined that he'd stiffened slightly as he'd spoken. What he'd said had been perfectly reasonable, but it was so unlike Matt to be reserved and somehow remote from her this way. She looked at him, trying to fathom what lay in the depths of those haunted, deep, blue eyes, but his thoughts were closed to her, and that bothered her more than she cared to admit.

'It's your mother, isn't it?' she said at last. 'She doesn't want anything to do with my family, does she? She blames my father for what's happened, and my mother and I are being dragged into that by association.'

His shoulders lifted, but he didn't try to deny it. 'She'll come around, sooner or later, but for now it's best not to stir things up, I think. She'll only be resentful, and I don't want to subject you to that.'

'I know,' she said on a sigh. 'I understand, I think…but I'm sorry it's come to this. I wish my father had acted differently, but he's a business-man and, like I said before, he expects everyone to have the same drive and ambition that he has. He sees things in terms of production and profit. He's always been like that. I'm sure he didn't ex-pect anything like this to happen.'

'I know. He rang my mother this morning to pass on his good wishes. She didn't want to speak to him, so I took the call for her.' His dark brows drew together as a monitor bleeped in the dis-tance. 'I have to go and see to that. You should go and prepare for your exam, Lucy. I'll see you later.'

Sadness clutched at her, settling deep in the pit of her stomach, making her tense. Somehow he had withdrawn from her in these last few hours, and it felt as though the easy friendship they had shared up to now was marred, shattered by these latest events. She didn't know what to do. It made her ache inside to see Matt brace his shoulders and move away from her. It came as a shock to discover how deeply she cared for him, and it was only now that she was beginning to realise just how much he meant to her. She didn't want to see their relationship fractured.

Those thoughts stayed with her as she went to meet Jade, but all too soon it was time for them to set off for the building where the final exams were to be held, and she made a determined effort to push everything else to the back of her mind.

'Good luck,' she said to Jade, giving her a hug. 'I'll see you back here when it's all over.'

'You, too.' Jade pulled a face, and they went off to find the first of their assessment stations. For the next few hours they would move from one station to another at five-minute intervals, except for a couple of examinations which would last for fifteen minutes, where they were expected to take a patient history and make a more detailed analysis of the situation.

'Your patient requires sutures to a hand wound,'

the female examiner said in this first session, and Lucy looked around the room. Of course there was no patient, only specialised material for her to work on. There was a suture pack laid out on the table, along with sterile gloves and everything that she needed to complete the task. What could go wrong? She knew how to do this, but she only had five minutes to show it. She took a deep breath, and explained what she was about to do. Then she opened the suture pack and put on the gloves, ready to make a start.

She had only managed to do two stitches when a bell rang out, signalling the time had come to an end. That should have been enough to show the examiner that she could do the task, so she dropped the needle into the sharps bin, thanked the woman and left the room, moving on to the second station. So far, so good.

'This patient is complaining of palpitations,' the next examiner said, and for a second or two Lucy's mind went blank. Palpitations…heart problems? She took a brief history from the woman who was simulating being a patient, and listened to her chest with her stethoscope. No heart problem there.

'What is the differential diagnosis?' asked the examiner.

Lucy thought about what Matt had said. *You get points for each step along the way...* So she listed the alternatives—stress, panic attacks, thyroid problems, and so on—and concluded with arrhythmia. 'I would need to take blood samples for testing to exclude or confirm these diagnoses and do an ECG,' she told the examiner, but of course there was no time for that, because when five minutes was up she had to move on once again.

It was stressful, and she was alert and running on adrenaline for the whole of the afternoon, but by the time the practical exams had finished she hoped she had done enough to pass. She wouldn't know the result for another week.

'How did it go?' she asked Jade when they met up for coffee in the cafeteria at the end of the session.

'Okay, I think,' Jade answered cautiously.

'There was one examiner who seemed a little uptight and kept barking questions at me, but I think I managed to keep cool and answer properly without getting flustered. And one of the patients kept arguing with me the whole time I was with her.' She shook her head. 'Perhaps she was asked to act up to see how we handle difficult patients.'

Lucy gave a small shudder. There had been one or two hiccups in her meetings with patients that she still found worrying. 'I'm glad it's over with, anyway. Are you thinking of heading for home now?'

'No. Actually, I said I'd meet Ben at the pub at the Bankside. We both have time off this weekend, so we're going to get something to eat and then drive over to my mother's house to sort out a few glitches in the wedding arrangements— there's been a last-minute hitch with the caterers so we have to choose a different menu and the bakery is querying the order for the cake.'

'Nothing too difficult, then,' Lucy said, smiling. 'I'll walk with you, if you like.'

'That'd be great. I was hoping you would stay and eat with us.'

'Oh, no…I wouldn't want to play gooseberry.'

Jade's mouth curved. 'You'd never be that. Anyway, Matt will be there. Ben rang me a few minutes ago to find out how the exams went. He said he'd met up with him after work, or, at least, Ben finished work and Matt had just come from seeing his father. He thought Matt needed cheering up, so he persuaded him to go along with him. We'll make up a foursome.'

'Okay…' Lucy said slowly. 'As long as Matt's going to be there, too.' She wasn't altogether sure Matt would be in any mood for a get-together, but since it looked as though it had all been arranged, she might as well go along with it. Actually, as Ben and Matt knew the girls were together, they'd probably worked out that it would be a good idea for them all to meet up.

The pub was in an ideal setting, by the river Thames. It was really old, dating back some eight hundred years, a grey stone building with brightly painted windows and flower baskets adding bold colour. There were tables and chairs set out on a paved area by the river bank, and inside there were wooden beams, ships' lanterns and old cider flagons set out on high shelves. It looked good, steeped in history, but Ben waved a hand towards the roof terrace and said, 'Shall we see if we can find a table up there?'

They all agreed it was the best idea, to take advantage of the summer sunshine, and after they'd all taken a look at the menu and decided what they wanted to eat, Ben and Jade went to the bar to place their orders.

It was a popular inn, frequented by office workers, professional people and tourists, and Lucy even saw a friend sitting at a table on the terrace, another fifth-year medical student. They waved to one another and signalled their relief at the end of the dreaded exams.

It was warm outside, the blue of the sky broken only by cotton-wool clouds, and from the roof terrace there was a wonderful view over the river. From here Lucy could see a good deal of the city...there was the magnificent dome of St

Paul's cathedral and the great Tower Bridge. She watched the river craft slowly edging towards it and then disappearing into the distance.

Matt came to sit beside her, following her glance across the water to the opposite bank. She pointed to the horizon and said softly, 'You could see the Great Fire of London from here, apparently. I read about this place. The writer, John Evelyn, came to the pub with his family and wrote about it. And they say that Samuel Pepys was a regular here, too—I know he wrote in his diary about the fire, and of coming to see it, but I don't know if he was at this pub on that particular night when the city burned.'

'It's hard to imagine, isn't it?' Matt remarked. 'It must have lit up the sky for miles around.'

Lucy glanced at him. He seemed to have relaxed a little, and she was pleased about that. He'd hardly spoken since they'd met up a short time ago, except to ask her how the exam had gone, but perhaps this historic place was working some kind of healing magic on him. She didn't want to spoil any of that by asking him about his father, but it would have been remiss not to say anything.

'Is there any news from the hospital?' she asked.

'Some. My dad's on medication to reduce the blood clot, of course, but the consultant told us he's planning to do a coronary angioplasty to widen the artery and improve the blood flow. It'll be a lot better for Dad than having to undergo heart bypass surgery, anyway. I don't know quite when they'll do it. I suppose it depends on how strong he is…how well he'll withstand the procedure.'

'How has your mother taken it?'

'All right, I think. She feels a bit better now that he's able to talk a little. It means that he's making some kind of a recovery, but of course these next few days are critical.'

Lucy laid her hand on his. 'Mr Sheldon's a brilliant man. He'll take good care of him.'

'I know. It's just that it's…it's still worrying when it's your own dad that's ill.'

'I know.' She wanted to put her arms around

him and hold him close, but this was hardly the place to do it, with so many people all around.

Jade and Ben came back, and after they'd chatted for a few minutes the waitress brought their meals to the table. Lucy tucked into lasagne, and she noted that Matt was eating beer-battered fish and chips, taking his time but gradually making inroads into his meal.

'So, how are your plans for the wedding coming along?' she asked, looking at Ben and Jade. 'In general, apart from the minor glitches, I mean. Will you be moving into the house when you come back from your honeymoon?'

'That's what we're hoping to do,' Ben said, tasting a portion of succulent gammon and smiling his satisfaction. 'It should be ready in time. There's only a bit of decorating to be finished off, some walls to be painted in the hall and up the stairs. You and Matt will have to come to our housewarming once we've settled in.'

'I'd love that,' Lucy said with a smile, taking a sip from her glass of chilled white wine. 'You've worked so hard on it between you, you must be longing to move in.' Matt murmured agreement.

Ben nodded. 'Just as soon as we have the wedding out of the way.' He glanced at Jade. 'The biggest problem we're having at the moment is seeing if we can get Jade's father to walk her down the aisle.'

'He seems to have fallen off the radar somehow,' Jade explained. She frowned, her fork hovering over her dish of pasta. 'I've been doing my best to get in touch with him, but so far I've had no luck. My brothers have been trying, as well, but they're coming up blank, too.'

'If we can't find him, Jade's stepfather will do the honours, so it's not a major calamity. It's just that having her father there would have been the icing on the cake for Jade.' Ben squeezed Jade's hand lightly, and she smiled at him, love shining in her eyes.

'If he were to come to my wedding, it would bring him back into the fold, I think,' she explained. 'He was away from us for so long when we were growing up, but I know he felt sorry about that and wanted to be closer to us. It's just that he's not answering my calls or my letters, so I'm not sure what's happened to him.'

'I hope things work out for you,' Lucy said sincerely.

They finished eating, and after a while Jade and Ben decided it was time that they started out for Jade's home in Amersham. 'We'll see you late on Sunday,' Jade said, giving Lucy a hug. 'Thank heaven those exams are over. I'm feeling quite light-headed all at once.'

'Enjoy your weekend,' Matt said.

They watched their friends go, and Lucy said in a low voice, 'We should do something about getting them a wedding present. The wedding will be on us before we know it.' She bit her lip. 'I'll be going home to spend the weekend with my parents, though, so it's going to be difficult to find the time.'

'And I'm on duty at the hospital. What about Monday? Do you have any free time then? I'll have the afternoon off.'

'That sounds good to me. We don't have any lectures now that the exams are over.'

She leaned back in her seat. Matt didn't show any sign of wanting to leave the pub, and Lucy was content with that. She liked being there with him.

'Would you like another drink?' he asked, and when she opted for a second glass of chilled white wine, he left her and went to the bar.

Lucy glanced around, catching sight of her medical-student friend once more. It looked as though the girl and her companions were getting ready to leave. They exchanged smiles once more, and on her way out the girl stopped by the table, sliding into the empty seat beside her. 'It's getting busy in here, isn't it?' she said. 'They must all be like us, wanting to let their hair down after a hectic week.' She laughed. 'Except that we've had more than a week of it, haven't we? I'm glad today's over and done with.'

'I know what you mean,' Lucy agreed. 'Did you get the examiner who seemed determined to catch people out?'

'I did. She really put me through it.' The girl made a face and then stood up. 'I must go. My friends will be waiting for me.'

'Okay, see you.' Lucy gazed around once more. It wouldn't be long before the empty table was filled. There were lots of tourists here, keen to lap up the ambiance of this pub at the centre of Victorian England, and even now she saw a group of people walking onto the roof terrace. She heard snatches of conversation, laughter, and as she glanced towards the steps once more she caught the sound of her own name being spoken. She froze. That voice had a familiar ring to it.

'Lucy?' A tall man, dark haired, immaculately dressed in a grey business suit, was with the group of people heading for the empty table in the corner of the terrace. His jacket hung open because of the heat of the day, and beneath it he wore a fine linen shirt. He walked towards her. 'It's good to see you. How are you? It's been a long time. Too long.'

'Hello, Alex.' She managed to find her voice. 'I'm fine, thanks. How are you?'

'Much better for seeing you.' He sat down next to her. 'I hope your girlfriend doesn't mind me taking her chair for a minute or two.' He smiled. 'I've been in London for about three months, now—I've been trying to call you, but you must have changed your number. I was hoping I might bump into you one day.'

'We both lead busy lives, I guess.' Her mind was reeling with the shock of seeing him. She'd imagined that he still lived in Berkshire.

He leaned closer, his hand resting on the back of her seat. 'Maybe you and I could get together one day? I felt really bad about what happened between us. I always knew, deep down, you were the only girl for me. I made a stupid mistake.' He hesitated, looking at her earnestly, his face just inches away from hers. 'Let me make it up to you.'

That was never going to happen. She gave a slight shake of her head, her mouth making a downward curve. Out of the corner of her eye, she saw Matt coming towards them, carrying two glasses. 'It's too late for that, Alex,' she said in a sober voice. 'We've both moved on since then.'

'Not me. I can't move on, Lucy…not without you.' He grasped her hand, cupping it with his own, and her heart sank. This was how he'd been before, never wanting to let go after she'd ended their relationship. It was only after she'd moved into her father's student house and had taken up placements at the local hospital that she'd managed to evade him. She'd even had to change her phone number.

'I'm sorry,' she said, trying to draw her hand away from his. She glanced at Matt as he reached the table. 'I'm not a free agent any more,' she stated clearly, turning her attention back to Alex. 'I have a boyfriend.' She waved a hand towards Matt, hoping that he would play along. 'So, you see, I'm not looking to start over.'

Matt's gaze narrowed. He placed the glasses on the table and said in a firm tone, 'I think, perhaps, introductions are in order?'

'Matt, this is Alex Ryder,' she said quickly. 'He used to work for my father.'

'I see.' He laid an arm around her shoulders. 'I have a feeling there's something I'm missing here.' He studied Alex as though he was sizing him up. 'Were you and Lucy an item at one time?'

'I… Yes…that's right…' Alex hastily pulled his hand away from hers as though it was scorching him. 'We were together for a couple of years when she first started medical school.'

'Really?' Matt frowned. 'It's a good thing that's well and truly over with, then, because, as she said, Lucy's with me now. Has been for some time.'

Lucy slowly exhaled, relief washing over her. Alex was still seated, but under Matt's penetrating stare he became uncomfortable and after a second or two he stood up.

'I… Perhaps I should go,' he said, looking hot under the collar. 'I'm glad you're okay, Lucy.'

She nodded. 'Goodbye, Alex.'

Alex moved away, going over to the table in the corner to join his friends, and Lucy looked up at Matt. 'Thank you for that,' she said. 'It was a tricky situation.'

'So I gathered.' He kept his arm around her. 'We've been in this situation before,' he commented dryly, 'with me stepping in at an opportune moment. Perhaps we should make an announcement—Matt and Lucy are an item.'

She laughed. 'Well, there's a thought.'

His gaze trailed over her and he smiled. 'Oh, yes. Definitely.' He didn't say any more, but slowly released her and came to sit down beside her at the table. Lucy was bemused. She never knew whether Matt was for real or whether he was teasing her.

Would it be such a bad idea if they were to be 'an item,' as he put it? She was finding more and more that she wanted to be with him all the time. And yet that was madness, wasn't it? Hadn't she had her fingers burned already? Why would Matt turn out to be any different from all the other men who simply wanted to get her into bed? He hadn't made any moves in that direction so far, but it could be that living in her father's house made him cautious. He knew how difficult her father could be regarding the men in her life.

'So tell me about this Alex,' Matt said, sitting down and swallowing his drink. 'He obviously still hankers after you. What did you do to him to put him in such a tizzy?'

'Me?' She stared at him wide-eyed. 'Nothing. It was the other way round.'

He paused, his glass an inch or so from his lips. 'Is he the one who managed to turn you off men?'

'I wouldn't say I was off men, exactly...I just had a bad experience and I went off the whole dating game for a while. You could say I was disillusioned.'

'Hmm.' He took another swallow. 'So who is he? Is he the one who caused you all those problems?' He put his glass down and looked her over. 'You were as white as a sheet when he was sitting down next to you. What happened with him? You said you were together for a couple of years, so there must have been some kind of rapport.'

'To begin with, yes, there was.' She toyed with her wine glass and then lifted it to her lips and drank as though she needed its invigorating strength. 'He's an architect, and he did quite a lot of work for my father, designing extensions to buildings, organising renovations and so on. That's how we met—I'd go home for the occasional weekend, and he would be at the house.' She gave a wry smile. 'I think my father arranged things that way. He was always vetting the men in my life, but he seemed to think Alex was the one for me, and he made a point of getting us together. To his mind, Alex had the right background, good manners and he seemed personable. So he was really pleased when Alex asked me out. I thought Alex was okay, so I agreed. It all started from there.'

He frowned. 'But it all went wrong?'

'Yes.' She began to fidget. 'Do you think we could get out of here? I can feel him staring at me. I'd like to go.' She drained the last of her wine, and looked at Matt.

'Sure.' He was already getting to his feet, and now he reached for her hand and drew her up from her chair. 'Your wish is my command, princess.'

She shot him a quick glance. She wasn't sure how to take that. Was he poking fun at her again? He seemed serious enough, though, and after a minute or two, when they were walking along the path by the river, she began to relax a little.

It was late evening by now, and a gentle breeze was blowing in off the river, riffling through her hair. Matt glanced at her, watching as she tucked the errant strands behind her ear.

'Are you feeling better now?' he asked. 'At least the colour's back in your cheeks.'

'I'm fine.'

'Good. So, do you want to tell me what happened with Alex?'

She pulled in a deep breath. 'Nothing too unexpected. He was all over me to begin with, even though I was cautious. He bought me flowers, small gifts, anything to try to win me round, but he was always a bit over the top, I thought. I got the feeling he liked being with the boss's daughter, that I was some sort of prize. He kept talking about getting engaged… I just wondered occasionally if marrying into a wealthy family was more important to him than I was. But he could be funny, and charming, and bit by bit I was beginning to think the two of us might make a go of it.'

She hesitated, thinking back to that time, and her vision clouded. 'It took a while before I realised I'd made a mistake.'

'He must have put a foot wrong, somewhere along the line,' Matt remarked.

She shrugged. 'It was partly my fault, I think. My career was important to me, and I was working really hard, studying, wanting to do well. He didn't understand that. He said I didn't need to do it when I could work for my father and not have to worry about anything.'

'But, of course, you couldn't do that?'

'No. He obviously didn't know me very well. Even though I'd tried to explain, he had no real idea how much it meant to me to break away and do what was really important to me. So I carried on studying and he went off and amused himself in the meantime.'

'Ah…' Matt watched her closely. 'By that you mean he found another woman?'

'Women. He played around, and I only found out about it when I dropped by his flat unexpectedly one day and caught him in bed with a girl who worked at the local store. And then I found a receipt for a necklace he'd bought for someone—his sister told me he'd given it to an old flame.' She gave a heavy sigh. 'I felt humiliated, and embarrassed because I was naïve enough to be fooled that way. I'm still embarrassed about it to this day.'

'There's no reason for you to feel that way. He's a jerk.' Matt put his arm around her and drew her close. 'I'm sorry that happened to you, Lucy.' He looked around, and waved a hand towards a building in the distance. 'If I had my way, that's where he'd be.' He smiled grimly. 'Only I'd have it in its original state, not the way it is now.'

He was pointing to the Clink Museum, the site of the old prison where, years ago, ne'er-do-wells had spent their time contemplating their sins. She laughed. 'You'd have him thrown in the clink—that's a bit drastic, but I like it.'

'It's ironic, isn't it?' he mused, 'that a man your father actually approved of should turn out to be so wrong for you?'

'It just goes to show that my father's only human,' she said. 'Sometimes he gets things wrong.'

He nodded. 'I wonder if he's come to realise he was wrong to expect you to stay in the family business? What does he think, these days, about you becoming a doctor?'

'He doesn't talk about it. But I suppose he gets to hear about what I'm up to from my mother. I call her regularly and let her know what's going on. She's been worrying about the exams and asking how the revision was going. I've no idea what my father thinks about it, apart from the fact he thinks I can spend time on his projects, as well as doing my revision.' She shrugged. 'Perhaps that says it all.'

'Maybe.' His glance ran over her. 'So you'll be

able to put your mother's mind at rest now that it's all over bar the waiting?'

Her mouth curved. 'Well, maybe she'll be relaxed about it—as long as I leave a few things out in the telling.'

They'd reached a quiet part of the walkway by now, and came to stand by railings, looking out over the river. Dusk was falling, and the branches of a tree nearby swayed gently in the faint breeze. The silver moon cast its beams on the water, sprinkling a myriad of sparkling gems over its surface.

Matt sent her a quizzical glance. 'What do you mean?' he asked. 'You said there were a couple of things that bothered you—I took it to mean that there were questions you had trouble with. Was I right? That won't necessarily mean that you've failed.'

'I hope not…only I did mess up a couple of times.'

'What happened?'

She pulled in a quick breath. 'One time, I had to test some blood and urine samples and the examiner kept barking questions at me, and had me so flustered at one stage that I almost knocked them over.' She gave a small shudder. 'But that wasn't the worst of it.' She sighed, thinking back over the afternoon.

Matt put his arms around her. 'It can't have been too bad, can it? From what you told me earlier, things seemed to have gone quite well.'

'Yes, but I didn't tell you about the CPR test, did I?' He shook his head, and she went on, 'There was a medical dummy in the room, a manikin, and the examiner said, "This man has collapsed. What will you do?" So I checked for signs of life and called for a crash team. Then I set to and started chest compressions, just as we've been taught, fifteen compressions, two ventilations. I did two cycles of that and then checked for signs of life again. The examiner came closer to see what I was doing. He was bending over to one side of me as I started the next lot of compressions, and maybe I was too vigorous or something, I don't know, but the manikin's arm suddenly shot up and smacked him in the face.'

'You're joking!' Matt choked.

'I'm not. I wish I was. But that's not all of it. I said, "Oh, I'm sorry. Have I broken it?" And he was holding his nose and said, "No, I don't think it's too bad. It's probably just bruised." And I said, "Um… I was talking about the manikin."'

Matt started to laugh. 'Oh, Lucy, you're price-less. I hope he has a sense of humour.'

'So do I. But I'm not sure really. He just grunted something and then the bell went and I had to move on to the next station.'

He was still laughing and she gave him a play-ful punch on the arm. 'It isn't funny…well, maybe a bit, but it wasn't at the time.'

He wound his arms more tightly around her and drew her to him. 'I'll keep a lookout for a con-sultant with a black and blue nose, and I'll know exactly who to blame if he fails you.'

He looked down at her, smiling, his face shad-owed in the moonlight, but she could see the glit-ter of his eyes, and her gaze was so intent on him that she saw the precise moment when laughter turned to contemplation and then slid into passionate intent.

His head lowered, he came closer, so close that his lips were just a breath away from hers, and then, after what seemed to Lucy like an achingly long time, he kissed her, tenderly at first and then as the fever took hold of him he deepened the kiss and his lips pressured hers, tasting, exploring, drinking from her as though she was the fountain of life itself. He eased her backwards against the trunk of the nearby tree, his long body following, moving against her, his thighs tangling with hers, so that sensation after sensation burst in small explosions all over her body, wherever they touched.

It took her breath away. Matt was kissing her, shaping her body with his hands as though he couldn't get enough of her, and she realised that she wanted this, needed it, in fact. She clung to him, kissing him fiercely in return, loving every moment, her body on fire where his hands caressed her, seeking out every dip and curve. She couldn't get enough of him, and he, it seemed, would not be satisfied until he'd kissed every inch of her bare skin, his lips gliding over her throat, the creamy slopes of her shoulders, nudging aside the thin straps of her cotton top, and then returning to dip down and discover the gentle swell of her breasts.

She was aching with need, and reached up to run her fingers through the silky hair at the nape of his neck. A soft groan rumbled deep in his throat, and he said raggedly, 'I've wanted to do this for so long. I've longed to hold you and kiss you like this. You can't imagine how difficult it's been, keeping away from you, when all I wanted to do was hold you in my arms.'

She whispered softly, 'Why did you hold back?'

He sighed, bending his head so that his cheek lay against hers. 'All sorts of reasons...and all of them are just as valid now. I shouldn't have done this...I know I shouldn't...but I couldn't help myself.'

Voices sounded on the night air, and Lucy came to her senses, shocked by the intrusion, and realised that they were out in the open, where people could disturb them at any minute. Matt eased himself away from her, holding her at arm's length as though he couldn't quite bring himself to let her go.

Then a group of young people came to look at the river, and Matt drew her away, walking with her through the quiet streets. They didn't talk much, each busy with their own thoughts.

Matt was right, of course. There were all sorts of reasons why they shouldn't be together, and looming largest among them was his family. His mother was going through a bad time, blaming Lucy's father for what had happened to her husband. She would be horrified to know that Matt was involved with her in any other way than as a tenant of the house where they both lived.

There was no way Lucy could put that right. She had spoken to her father, warned him what might happen, but he had ignored her pleas.

And now circumstances had overtaken them, and Matt's father was desperately ill, just when she had discovered what it was that she really wanted.

She wanted Matt. More than that, she loved him.

CHAPTER SEVEN

'OKAY, so which song would you like me to play for you next?' It was Matt's voice, coming from the central area of the children's ward.

Intrigued, Lucy walked towards the nurses' station and saw Matt, sitting on a straight-backed chair, strumming his guitar in front of a rapt audience of children.

The children called out or stuck their hands in the air, all clamouring at once for his attention, and it seemed the majority vote was for a pop song heading the charts right now. Matt cheerfully obliged. He sang, as well as played, and Lucy's legs turned to jelly as she listened to the throbbing lilt of the melody.

He was pitch perfect, and his voice was so sexy, so expressive that she started to come out in goose bumps all over. He'd mastered guitar playing so well that it seemed as though the music was an integral part of him. She closed her eyes and listened, letting the sound flow all around her. It was heavenly. She could have listened to him forever.

But the song came to an end all too soon. A ward assistant brought a trolley round, loaded with milky drinks, and began to serve them to the children, while Mandy started a second round of blood-pressure and temperature checks.

'I'll play some more for you later,' Matt responded to the children who wanted him to go on with the impromptu concert. 'I have to go and look after those youngsters who are too poorly to listen to music.' He smiled, and ruffled the hair of a boy who came and asked if he could try the guitar for himself. 'Two minutes, then,' Matt said, 'and after that you must hop back into bed or Mandy will be telling me off. I'll let you have another go later on.' He handed the guitar to the twelve-year-old, who plucked happily at the strings for a while.

Matt caught sight of Lucy, waiting by the desk,

and his smile instantly made her light up inside. 'It's good to see you,' he said as she walked towards him. 'How are you doing?'

'Suffering from lack of sleep,' she answered ruefully. 'I came home late last night from my parents' house and could have slept for a week. As it was, I snoozed all through the first alarm and couldn't believe it when the second one started shrieking in my ear. I think all my adrenaline's run out now that the exams are over and the medical school term is almost finished.'

'You must have needed the rest,' he murmured, scooting the boy back to bed and placing his guitar behind the desk. He turned to give Lucy his full attention. 'How are you getting on with your father?'

'We're all right, but it would be better for me if I weren't so reliant on him,' she said cautiously, following Matt to a treatment bay.

'You mean, because he pays for the roof over your head?'

She nodded. 'If I pass my exams and become a qualified doctor, at least I'll be able to start paying him back. And he'll be less likely to drop things on me at a moment's notice…or try to check on the men in my life.'

He shook his head. 'I don't think that's going to happen. He loves you. Whatever he does, it's because he cares about you.'

'Even though I didn't stay with the family firm?' Her voice took on a cynical edge. 'I let him down. I don't think he's going to forget that in a hurry.'

'Well, you never know. He might respect you for making a stand.'

'And one day pigs might fly.'

'And that, too.' He laughed. 'Anyway, we've work to do. If we stand here much longer, people will think we've given up on medicine altogether.'

'Yes, you're right.' She looked around, dragging her mind back to the work at hand. 'Are we going to take a look at the new admission?'

'Yes.' Matt was already leafing through the infant's chart. 'Alice Jackson…two-and-a-half years old.' He frowned. 'Her mother says she's been generally unwell, lethargic, with abdominal cramps and irritability. She cries a lot. There seems to be some muscle weakness, too.' He pulled in a deep breath. 'Let's go and find her.'

A couple of minutes later Lucy looked down at the infant in the cot. 'Poor little mite.' The toddler was whimpering to herself, clearly unhappy, her cheeks tear-stained. 'We'll have to hurry up and find out what's going on with you, won't we?' She turned to Matt. 'From the looks of her, she's dehydrated. Shall I set up a normal saline line?'

'Yes, just as soon as I've finished checking her over.' Matt ran his stethoscope over the girl's chest, and when he'd finished he moved to one side to allow Lucy to listen to her chest.

'Her heart rate's seems to be slow,' Lucy said, concentrating on the heartbeat. 'I think we should do an ECG.'

He nodded. 'That was my thought, too. Her blood pressure's high.' He put his stethoscope away and wrote the figures down on the girl's chart. 'We'll get some blood and urine tests done, and see what they come up with.'

Lucy set up the ECG and waited for the print-out that would show them if the child's heart was behaving normally.

A few minutes later she tore off a section of the printout and showed it to Matt. 'The heart-beat is definitely irregular,' she pointed out. 'It's too slow. Could there be a problem with the heart muscle, one that's disrupting the electrical signals?'

'It's possible. We'll wait and see what results we get from the tests then we'll be able to decide on a course of action.'

'Okay, what next?'

He glanced at his watch. 'I'm going over to Neonatal to check up on baby Sarah—I'm keeping my fingers crossed that there have been no more setbacks. Her parents can't take much more. They're already worrying about brain damage.' He brooded on that for a moment, and then said, 'I think we'll probably try taking her off the ventilator some time this week. She hasn't had any more seizures and she's managed to put on a little weight. We'll just have to see how it goes and hope that she can manage to breathe on her own.'

'I thought she had a little more colour in her cheeks when I looked at her first thing this morning,' Lucy commented. She glanced around the ward. 'What would you like me to do? I looked in on Tom, the five-year-old, earlier this morning.' The boy's grandmother was still arguing with her son-in-law, and Lucy shuddered inwardly. She felt for the boy's mother. She would hate to have her relationship marred in that way, with the people she loved most at odds with each other. An image of Matt and her father flitted through her mind, only to be replaced by one of Matt's mother frowning at the thought of any liaison between Lucy and her son. It was as though they were doomed at the outset.

She cut off those thoughts and turned her attention back to work. 'The neurosurgeon drained some of the excess fluid from his brain, and he's just waiting to see if he responds to the medication.'

'Hmm. That could take some time.' He glanced

through the files on the nearby desk. 'You could look in on young William and take his stitches out. He seemed a lot better yesterday, so with any luck we can get him up and about in a few days. Once his blood count has stabilised he'll be able to go home.'

'All right.' She nodded. 'I can do that.' She sent him a quick look. 'Are we still on for that trip to the shops this afternoon? I thought maybe Jade and Ben might like to have something special, like a set of crystal wine glasses or a beautiful ornament for their new house. They probably have all the basics already, like towels, duvets, microwave oven, and so on.'

'Yes, of course. I'll have to come back to the hospital to look in on my father when we've finished, though. He really looks forward to having visitors, even though he gets tired afterwards. He hates being cooped up in hospital, but he's too ill to fight it.' He smiled. 'I'll come and find you as soon as I've finished in Neonatal—and I just want to take a quick look at William before we go. Crystal sounds good.'

He left the ward, and Lucy went to look in on the ten-year-old who'd come in after the traffic accident a few weeks ago and ended up needing to go to Theatre for an emergency repair to his spleen.

Now he was sitting up in bed, and she was pleased to see that he looked much brighter today.

'Hi, William,' she greeted him. 'How are you doing?'

'Okay.' He shrugged. 'The doctor said I was going to have my stitches out today.' He sent her a guarded look. 'Will it hurt?'

Lucy smiled and shook her head. 'No. You'll be fine. I'm going to do it myself. I promise you I'll be very gentle and you'll hardly know I'm doing it.'

He cheered up at that, and showed her the game he was playing on his hand-held console. 'I'm on level ten,' he told her.

'Level ten? Heavens, you're good, aren't you?' She pulled a face. She'd borrowed Matt's console last week so that she could have a go, but her efforts were dismal by comparison. 'I only managed to get to level five,' she told him. 'And now Dr Berenger keeps telling me he's the man, 'cos he reached level ten, same as you.'

William laughed. 'I like him. He's way good on the guitar, and he brings me comic books and talks to me about football and stuff.'

'Yes, I've noticed… He always has something or other in his pockets, doesn't he? I expect he'll be along to see you before he goes off for lunch. He'll want to check your operation scar.' She watched him play the game for a few minutes and then went to gather together what she needed to remove the boy's sutures.

'This is easy-peasy,' she told him, as she set out her sterile pack. 'You'll feel a slight pulling sensation, that's all. I'm going to clean the area first of all, so you just have to lie back and relax. Watch television while I do it, if you like.'

'Yeah,' he said, looking up at the screen. '*Robots on Planet Mars* is just starting. That's well good.'

She smiled. It was good to see him looking perky after all he'd been through.

When she had finished removing all the stitches, William looked down at her handiwork. 'That didn't take long,' he commented. 'Mum will be surprised when she comes back from having lunch. She didn't know I was having them out.' He frowned. 'Do you think there'll be a scar?'

Lucy studied the line of stitching. 'Just a faint line, perhaps. I think you'll still be just as handsome and wow the girls.'

He grinned. 'Oh, yeah.'

Matt came along and inspected the healed wound. 'That's looking good,' he said. 'We need to make sure you keep the area clean for a bit longer, so the nurse will come and put a dressing on it once your mother has had a chance to take a look. I think she'll be pleased. It's healthy looking, and the surgeon made a very neat job of it.'

They left William a few minutes later. 'I think we've done everything that was necessary,' Matt said, glancing at Lucy, 'and I've handed over to the registrar, so if you're ready, we can go.'

'I'm ready.' She collected her bag and they

headed out of the hospital. 'I think it might be best if we take the tube and head for Oxford Circus. There are a few department stores we could check out along Oxford Street.'

'Okay. That sounds good.'

Sometime later they emerged from the Underground and walked through the city streets, looking into shop windows, stopping every now and again to go inside a store and check out the glassware. Lucy bought a pretty jewellery box as a gift for her mother's birthday.

Outside, it was a clear, bright day, a little cooler than usual, but she breathed in the fresh air and was glad that Matt was by her side. He wore tailored grey trousers and a crisp shirt that matched the colour of his eyes. He'd undone the top buttons of his collar, and Lucy's gaze was drawn to the pale bronze of his skin. She yearned to gently trail her lips over his warm throat and feel the throb of his pulse against her cheek.

He sent her an oblique glance, a faint smile playing around his mouth, and a rush of heat flowed along her cheekbones. Had he seen her looking at him? He couldn't possibly know what she'd been thinking, could he?

'How about this store?' Matt said. 'There should be a pretty good selection of glassware in here. And then, when we've finished looking around, we could go up to the bistro and have some lunch. I'm starving.'

They stepped inside the department store, a complete contrast to the outside world. In here, everything glittered under the bright, artificial lighting, all the surfaces were smooth and polished, and the air was heavy with fragrance from the assortment of perfumes on sale. They took the escalator up to the third floor and wandered around the displays, mulling over vases and decanters and all types of sparkling crystalware.

'What about these?' Matt suggested, pointing out a set of beautiful, elegant champagne flutes with deeply etched lines and an embossed design.

Lucy gazed at them. 'Oh, yes. They're lovely. Absolutely perfect.'

They smiled at one another. 'That was easy enough,' Matt said. 'I thought we might be looking around all afternoon. As it is, we're all done and dusted and it's still not yet three o'clock. There's time for us to go and grab something to eat, and then we can explore for a bit, if you like.'

'Are you sure? What about your father? Will he be expecting you soon?'

He shook his head. 'The consultant will be looking in on him this afternoon, so I'll give him some space.' He gave her a quizzical look. 'Is there anything you'd like to see in particular?'

Lucy gave it some thought. 'The London Eye,' she said. 'I've always wanted to ride on it, but so far I've never had the chance.' She pulled a face. 'And I think usually there's quite a queue.'

'It may not be too bad. I'll phone ahead to see if I can book a couple of tickets—that way we might not have to wait so long.'

'That's a great idea.'

He made the booking then led the way to the bistro, where they had a late lunch, filling up on tapas dishes, delicious Spanish rice and prawns with onion, and spicy chicken wings with salad.

'Mmm…mmm…I love this food,' Lucy murmured, reluctantly putting down her fork, too full to eat any more and quenching her thirst with an ice-cold spritzer. 'This is turning out to be a great day. I never expected it somehow. It's funny how moods can be lightened with a bit of sunshine and retail therapy, isn't it?'

Matt's gaze meshed with hers. 'I think this is the first time in months that I've seen you looking so relaxed. It's good to see you this way.'

She was content for the first time in a long while. Matt knew everything about her. He looked beneath the surface and saw the woman with doubts and uncertainties, and he understood that she was cautious about men who only wanted her for the way she looked. She felt safe with him. She knew him, knew everything about him that was important, and she could easily imagine spending the rest of her life with him. It felt right, as though it was meant to be.

He held her hand as they left the bistro, and Lucy felt a warm surge of happiness flow through her. Maybe something would happen to bring her down to earth again before too long, but for now she was walking on air, and she was going to make the most of it.

They made their way to the London Eye, and she was surprised to discover that there wasn't a huge queue of people waiting to board. She stepped inside the capsule with Matt, and instead of going over to the central seating area they went to stand by the glass window so that they could enjoy the panoramic view of London.

Matt slipped his arm around her waist, and together they looked for the landmark buildings—the Houses of Parliament on the right, Big Ben, and to the east, St Paul's Cathedral and the 'Gherkin,' one of the tallest buildings in London. 'I love the way the sunlight reflects on the glass,' Lucy said. 'To me it's one of the most beautiful buildings in the city.'

'Mmm, you're right.'

She glanced at him. 'You're not looking at it,' she murmured. Instead, his gaze was fixed steadily on her, gliding over her long, golden hair and coming to rest on the full, pink curve of her mouth.

'That's because I'm feasting my eyes on something far more lovely,' he said huskily against her cheek. 'I just wish we were alone up here so that I could show you how good you make me feel.'

She snuggled into the crook of his arm and looked down at the river flowing beneath them. She wanted this moment to last forever but, of course, it couldn't.

They stepped out of the glass pod at ground level, and walked by the river for a while. The chimes of Big Ben rang out, and Lucy suddenly remembered that Matt had to go back to the hospital. A small wave of sadness hit her. She didn't want the afternoon to end.

Even so, she said, 'You're supposed to be visiting your father, aren't you? It's all right…I'll understand if you need to go.'

'Come with me,' he said.

'Are you sure?' Her heart gave a small leap in her chest. He must have changed his mind about keeping her away from his family and that was altogether reassuring. He was prepared to let his parents know that she was part of his life.

'I'm sure.'

They took the tube back to the hospital in order to save time. Matt was concerned about his father's condition, and as their destination drew closer, the quieter he became.

'Is he strong enough for the operation yet?' she asked, as they left the Underground and walked the short distance to the hospital.

'He's stronger than he was, so there's a good chance the consultant will do it within a few days,' he acknowledged. 'The trouble is, my father won't rest. Once he started to feel a bit better, he began to phone the office, checking up on how things were going. Some of his men were due to start work on the waterfront house, just as soon as the materials were delivered, and he's been agitating to give them the go-ahead. Of course, that means keeping an eye on things, making sure the job's done properly and with a decent time frame.'

'But he can't do that, surely?' Lucy was appalled that he would even consider it.

He pulled a face. 'You'd have thought not,

wouldn't you? But my father's never been one to stay idle, and he was getting himself worked up about things, so I had to step in. I told him I'd oversee the project and report back to him.'

'Matt, how on earth can you pull that off? You're working all hours. When you're not at the hospital, you're playing gigs somewhere or other—you need some time to yourself.' They went through the main doors of the hospital and made for the lift bay.

'I've been stopping by the house whenever I had the chance—like this weekend, after work, for instance.' He pressed the button for the lift. 'It's coming along okay, I think, but my father's still agitating. He can't bear to be out of things, away from where it's all going on.'

'I can see why he and my father get on—or rather, used to get on. I'm not sure how they feel about one another now, after what's happened… but they're two of a kind, aren't they? My father pushes, and yours can't say no.'

Matt acknowledged that with a smile. 'One thing's for certain, my dad is going to have to start saying no, or he'll be in deep trouble health-wise.'

By now they had reached his father's ward, and even before they reached his bed it was clear that all was not well. Sam was sitting up in bed, tapping the keyboard of a laptop and pausing every now and again to talk on his mobile phone. He looked harassed, out of breath, and the monitor beside him had started to bleep. Already Lucy sensed the tension building up in Matt.

'What do you think you're doing?' he demanded, going over to his father's bedside. 'Didn't I tell you there was to be no working while you were in hospital?' He glowered at the laptop. 'And what do I find the minute my back's turned?'

His father gave a guilty start. 'Oh, it's nothing.' He fought for breath. 'Just a small thing I needed to clear up.'

'There's no need for you to be clearing anything up. I told you I would deal with everything. I'm perfectly capable, or don't you trust me?'

'Of course I do, I...' He broke off, unable

to speak, and the display on the heart monitor started to show a chaotic, uncoordinated pattern.

'He's gone into V-fib,' Lucy cried, shocked. She called for a crash team at the same time as she saw Matt's father slump against his pillows. His heart had stopped pumping blood around his body, and instead it was quivering in a way that could lead to complete cardiac arrest. She quickly moved the laptop and phone out of the way.

Matt delivered a precordial thump to his father's chest, aiming to stimulate his heart into a normal rhythm, but although the monitor registered a correction for a short time, Sam's heart reverted back to ventricular fibrillation.

Matt began chest compressions, while the crash team prepared the defibrillator. He stood back while the registrar placed the paddles on his father's chest and delivered a shock to the heart. There was no change. The registrar gave Sam a second shock and as they all waited, silent, tense and alert, the monitor blipped and a normal rhythm was established.

Lucy sighed with relief and glanced at Matt. He

was drained of colour, standing there, not moving, and she went over to him and laid a hand on his shoulder, wanting to comfort him but conscious of everyone around them.

'He's back,' she said softly. 'It's over…you can relax now.'

He nodded, but still he didn't move. And then Lucy became aware that his mother had come into the room and was looking anxiously at her husband, taking in everything that had happened.

Lorraine Berenger turned to her son. 'It's that house,' she said. 'He's done nothing but work on it since he began to recover, and now look at him, barely hanging on to life.' Her shoulders sagged. 'I can't take much more of this.' Her expression was bleak, and Matt put an arm around her, drawing her close.

Lucy stepped back, out of the way. His mother's gaze followed her, flint sharp, bright with condemnation. She didn't say anything, but she didn't have to. Lucy knew that she blamed her every bit as much as her father for what had happened. The house was Lucy's project, but it had rapidly become Sam's.

'I'll go,' Lucy said softly.

'You don't need to do that. Stay…' Matt said, but seeing his mother's stony features Lucy shook her head.

'You need to be with your parents,' she murmured. 'I'll see you later, back at the house.'

'I don't know how long I'll be. You don't have to go,' Matt insisted.

'I know. That's all right. Don't worry about it.'

She left the room and walked back to the lift. She felt lonely, empty inside, as though she'd been cast adrift on a cold and choppy sea.

CHAPTER EIGHT

'Is THERE any news about your father?' Ben asked, helping himself to scrambled egg and glancing across the breakfast table towards Matt.

Lucy was spreading butter on her toast, but now she looked up, wanting to hear Matt's answer. More than a week had passed since his father's second collapse, and though she'd regularly asked him how he was doing, so far he'd been noncommittal.

She missed the closeness she'd shared with Matt. Between work, his visits to the hospital to see his father and the gigs that had come up of late, she hadn't been able to spend much time alone with him. And on those occasions when they had been together, Ben and Jade had also been in the house.

Perhaps it was just as well that things were

going this way. She longed for things to go back to how they had been before that fateful day, but his mother's reaction to her had shown her that there would always be a barrier to any relationship between her and Matt, especially if his father didn't recover.

'I think he's a little stronger now,' Matt answered. He lifted the coffee pot and looked at Lucy and Jade to see if they wanted their cups topped up. Lucy nodded, sliding her cup forward. 'The consultant is thinking about doing the coronary angioplasty in a couple of days,' he went on, as he poured coffee. 'Having a stent put in to widen the artery will certainly improve his quality of life, and as long as he stops working and gets all the rest he needs, he should do all right.'

Lucy smiled. 'You took his laptop off him, so that must have helped.'

'Yeah…' He grinned. 'And the nurses are monitoring his use of the phone. Not that he'll get any joy from ringing the office, anyway. I've put all the employees under strict instructions not to answer any of his calls. My brother's helping to keep an eye on that, too.'

'It's good news about the operation, anyway,' Lucy said. 'Your mother will be relieved, I imagine. Is she a bit more relaxed about the situation these days?'

'I'm not so sure about that.' He winced. 'She's been working on him to persuade him that he needs to break off the partnership and go it alone. He'd make a go of it because he has a full order book, but he's been with your father for a long time, and I think it would be a wrench for him to leave him behind.'

She drew in a ragged breath. It was much worse than she had imagined. 'I think it would be difficult for both of them after all these years.'

Jade drank her coffee and looked at Matt over the rim of her cup. 'With all this going on, how are you going to be fixed for our wedding? I know Ben wants you to be his best man more than anything.'

Ben nodded agreement. 'But if it's going to be a problem...'

Matt shook his head. 'It'll be fine. I've even been practising my speech—all those little jokes I have up my sleeve...'

Jade groaned. 'Oh, no, I don't think I want to hear this...'

'Are you sure?' Matt pretended to be disappointed.

'Quite sure.' She laughed, and then said quickly, 'Oh, and while I think of it, my brother James said he'll drive you both back here from Amersham on the night of the wedding, if you like. He and his fiancée live in London, and they have to come back the same day, so it won't be a problem.'

'That's great, thanks,' Lucy said, glancing at Matt to see if it was all right with him. He nodded.

'It'll save us having to get the train,' he commented.

Jade's phone started to ring, and she gave an apologetic smile and answered it. She listened for a moment and then said, 'You've seen them? What did it say? Did you check them all? Oh, wow. Oh, wow…' She clicked off the call a minute or so later and then turned to Lucy. 'The exam results are up on the notice-board in the lecture room,' she told her. 'We passed! Both of us! Oh, wow, wow!'

The two girls jumped up and held on to each other, dancing around the room for a few seconds, then Jade grabbed hold of Ben and kissed him soundly. 'I passed,' she said, her excitement still riding high. 'I passed.'

'Well, of course you did,' he answered calmly, but with a twinkle in his eye. 'What did you expect?'

Lucy was smiling at Matt, and he went over to her, wrapping his arms around her and holding her in a bear hug. 'Well done,' he said. 'I knew you could do it.' As soon as his arms went around her, Lucy's thoughts went into a tailspin. She wanted this, loved being in his arms, but something would surely go wrong. It had been a mistake, falling for Matt. It was a mistake, being in his arms like this. Their families were alienated and she felt responsible for some of that.

But all of that went out of her head when he leaned towards her and kissed her. It was a tender kiss at first, but soon he was moving in closer, deepening the kiss so that she was lost to all sensible thought, and all she wanted was for it to go on and on. Which it did, until they were both wrenched from their cosy little cocoon when they heard a round of applause coming from across the room.

'Well, there's a thing,' Jade said, trying to hide a smile and failing completely. 'I wondered how you two might be getting on in our absence. I thought you might be dividing the house into territories with a barrier in between to keep you apart, but this is good, very good.' She was grinning widely now, and so was Ben, and Lucy didn't know where to put her face. She was sure she was blushing fiercely.

'I'm glad things are working out for you two,' Ben said. 'But enough of this frivolity, I'm on duty in half an hour. I have to go.'

'Me, too.' Matt held Lucy for just a while longer, as though he couldn't bring himself to let go, but then he slowly released her and went to get ready for work.

Lucy dragged her mind back to mundane things, glad that Jade had gone to find her bag and she didn't have to talk to anyone just then. She'd been overwhelmed by that kiss, and now she had to shore up her defences all over again. She couldn't get involved with someone whose mother hated her and her family. It wouldn't be fair to Matt if he had to constantly work at keeping the peace between them. And sooner or later wouldn't it cause friction between them, too?

And what of Matt's feelings for her? Where was their relationship going? He'd kissed her, and he definitely cared for her, that was for sure, but he'd never actually spoken to her about how he felt. Perhaps she wanted more from him than he was prepared to give.

She broke up the remains of the toast into crumbs and then went out into the garden and dropped them onto the bird table, looking around as, out of the corner of her eye, she spotted a sleek white cat.

'He likes your garden,' a small voice said, and her glance flicked to where Jacob was peering at her, resting his chin on the top of the wooden fence.

'It looks like it, doesn't it?' The cat was searching in the undergrowth for a good place to settle down, and Lucy smiled, looking back at the boy. 'My word, you've suddenly grown,' she said, sounding astonished. 'Look at you, able to see over the fence. Have you been eating lots of dinners?'

Matt came to join her in the garden, and she pointed out the boy to him. 'He must have grown a foot in two weeks,' she mused.

'Hmm…strange, that,' Matt said on a thoughtful note. 'I've seen his mum watering the carrots with plant food just lately. I wonder if she's been watering him, as well?'

They both shook their heads in puzzlement, and Jacob giggled. 'I'm standing on a box,' he said, his voice rising with glee. 'A big wooden box.'

'Oh, well, that's it, then. And I thought you

were as big as the fence.' Lucy chuckled. She moved away from the bird table. 'We have to go to work now, Jacob.' She waved at him. 'Perhaps we'll see you later.'

'Okay.'

Matt put his arm around her as they walked back to the house. 'We should set off for the hospital,' he said. 'Jade and Ben have already gone.'

She nodded. With his arm around her shoulders and his body next to hers, she was in seventh heaven. The only thing that would have made it better would be for him to kiss her, but that wouldn't do at all, would it? She was having enough trouble getting over the last time.

She looked up at him, her blue eyes quizzical.

'Don't even think about it,' he said, his eyes gleaming. 'Or I won't be responsible for my actions.'

'I can't think what you mean,' she murmured. That last kiss had been a spur-of-the-moment thing, hadn't it? She couldn't read anything into it. Matt had been going through a rash of temptation lately, and it was only because they'd been thrown together over these last few weeks. He cared about her, but he didn't love her, did he? He'd never said that he loved her.

They walked to the hospital a few minutes later, and as soon as she entered the Neonatal unit Lucy's nerves were on edge. Matt was going to take baby Sarah off the ventilator this morning, and everything depended on whether she could breathe on her own.

Lucy looked at her, a tiny infant with thin little arms and legs, wearing a knitted cap to keep the warmth from escaping at the top of her head. Matt could probably hold her comfortably in one hand.

'Are you ready?' He looked at her, and he must have guessed that she was overwhelmed by misgivings. What if the baby couldn't breathe on her own? Would she be distressed, or choke? Just the thought of it bothered her.

'Yes, I'm ready.' She could do this…she had to do this. She'd almost finished her five years of medical training, she'd passed all her exams over the years, and now there was nothing standing in the way of her becoming a pre-registration doctor. She even had her next stage of training arranged—the first year of a three-year course to enable her to become a GP, a family doctor. How could she look anyone in the eye if she couldn't bear to watch a small baby being taken off a ventilator?

'Do you want to do it?' Matt asked. 'You've seen it done before, haven't you, and you've practiced on manikins before this? She'll be fine. We've been monitoring her all the while, and I feel she's ready for this. We'll continue with oxygen afterwards, but it'll be delivered through an oxygen tent rather than through a tube down her throat.'

'All right. I'll do it.'

She followed the procedure she'd been shown many times before, and switched off the machine before carefully withdrawing the tube. The baby coughed, retched and for a few interminable seconds seemed to choke, but Lucy was ready with suction to clear any secretions from her throat.

Then the infant took a spontaneous breath and began to wail lustily.

Lucy exhaled deeply. It had worked, and the baby was breathing by herself. She turned to Matt, her mouth curving in a relieved smile.

'That wasn't so bad, was it?' he said.

She shook her head. 'Now we have to wait and see how well she does on her own.' She frowned. 'We won't know the extent of any brain damage for some time, will we?'

He pressed his lips together briefly. 'We'll do a CT scan at some point. That will give us an idea of what's going on. But after suffering from bleeding on the brain, it's hard to imagine that there'll be no problems ahead. Anyway,' he said, becoming businesslike once more, 'in the meantime, we'll keep her on medication to regulate the heartbeat and watch to see if she starts to put on weight and generally gain strength.'

They left the Neonatal unit and went to check on their patients on the children's ward.

'I'll catch up with you in a few minutes,' Matt

said. 'I want to go and look up some X-ray films on the computer.'

'Okay. I'll go and see how Tom is doing.' She was worried about the boy with the head injury. He had a broken leg, too, and although it had been treated and put into a cast, the healing wouldn't be complete until he could start to put some weight on it.

She hesitated as she approached his bay, though, because she could hear raised voices coming from there.

'I wish your mother would keep her opinions to herself,' Tom's father was saying. 'She's always having a go at me.'

'It's only because she's upset, and worried about Tom,' his wife answered.

'Sure, make excuses for her, why don't you? That's all you ever do…side with her.'

'She's my mother, for heaven's sake. I don't want to take sides. I just want you both to sort yourselves out and let me concentrate on our child.'

Lucy closed her eyes briefly, trying to shut out

the image that circled in her mind. She didn't want to see or hear this couple arguing, especially when their child was so desperately ill. But neither could she rid herself of the other vision that rose up clear and sharp in her head. Was this how it would be for her and Matt? Would his mother's animosity taint any relationship they might have?

She walked towards the bedside, clearing her throat to alert the couple to her presence, and they both fell silent. 'I've come to see how Tom's getting on,' she said, glancing at the monitors and then leafing through the boy's file. 'Since the pressure inside his head has gone down, we've started to gradually reduce the sedation. He might start to show signs of coming round so you need to be aware and alert one of the nurses if that happens. It might not be very much, just be the twitch of a finger or a slight movement of his good leg to begin with.'

Mrs Granger brightened. 'That's all we need,' she said softly. 'Anything to give us a sign that he's coming back to us.'

'I don't think it will be too long now,' she told

them. She inspected the various catheters to make sure all was well, and then added a few notes to the boy's file before taking one final look at him. He wasn't moving, but he looked serene and peaceful.

Taking her leave of them, she went over to the nurses' station. She was looking through the wire tray on the desk for any test results that had come in when Matt came to join her.

'Alice's results are here,' she told Matt. 'The two-year-old with abdominal cramps and slow heartbeat,' she reminded him. 'The serum calcium and parathyroid hormone are both elevated, and serum phosphate is decreased. Sounds as though her parathyroid gland isn't working properly and she's overloaded with calcium. That means we should look out for kidney stones.'

He nodded. 'Let's go and take a look at her. We'll do a scan, but we can give her a potassium supplement to help prevent stones. She's still on normal saline, so we'll add a diuretic, furosemide, to help eliminate any excess calcium, and she'll need an injection of calcitonin to strengthen her bones.'

She walked with him to the child's cot. 'Should we try her on bisphosphonates to stop the breakdown of bone?'

'Yes. You can set up an infusion.' He looked at the infant, an unhappy little girl, fretful and restless, and said softly, 'We'll soon have you feeling better, little one.' He stroked her hand and then waggled his fingers at her, making funny noises and puffing his cheeks so that after a while she stopped whimpering and began to chuckle. 'That's the way,' he murmured. 'I'll get the play leader to come and find something to amuse you.'

Turning back to Lucy, he said, 'I'll call for a consultation with the endocrinologist. If the illness is due to a problem with the parathyroid gland, such as a tumour of some kind, she'll need surgery.'

'Poor little thing. I hope we can sort her problems out fairly quickly.'

'So do I.'

Lucy's mobile phone rang at that moment, and

she went to a quiet corner of the room to answer it. Matt stayed where he was, setting up the child's medication.

'Dad, what is it?' she asked, concerned all at once. He sounded agitated. He rarely rang her at work, so something must be bothering him quite badly. 'Is everything all right? Is Mum okay?' Matt glanced at her, hearing the concern in her voice, and she lifted her shoulders in answer to his unspoken query, showing her bewilderment.

'She's fine,' her father said. 'It's this business with Matt's father I'm ringing about. Apparently, he's been talking to a lawyer about ending the partnership. I had a letter from the solicitor this morning. Can you talk to him for me? I can't reach him by phone, and his email's not working. As for his wife, she won't speak to me at all—she just puts the phone down on me. He can't be serious. I don't think he can have thought this through.'

'I'm sorry,' she said. 'It must have come as an awful shock to you. You've worked together for so long. How many years is it? About twenty?'

She looked at Matt, willing him to come over to her. This concerned him. It was about his father, after all.

Matt finished what he was doing and checked that everything was in order before he joined her in the seating area.

'It's about that, yes…a long time. I'm sure we could work something out between us. We've always worked well together, and I just don't want to lose him as a partner.' Beside her, Matt pulled in a deep breath. Clearly, he could hear what was being said. 'Will you talk to him for me, Lucy? See if you can get him to change his mind?'

'I don't see how I can do that,' Lucy said honestly. 'I get the feeling Matt's mother doesn't like me being there. And she's encouraging him to make the break so she won't thank me for going along and trying to persuade him otherwise.'

'You could try, though.'

She shook her head, even though he couldn't see her. 'I don't think so. It wouldn't have any weight coming from me, anyway. I don't have much to do with the business, apart from helping to find development sites and dealing with suppliers. I don't see what arguments I can put forward to persuade him to stay.'

He didn't like her answer. She knew it. She sensed his disapproval even before he spoke, and when he did, he ground his words out through his teeth. 'That's been the trouble all along, hasn't it? You never wanted to be part of the business. You insisted on going ahead with a career in medicine when you could have had a ready-made partnership on your doorstep. But, no, you took it into your head to take off instead and get yourself involved in years of study—expensive study, mind you—and for what? So that you can set yourself up as a family doctor and listen to people coming in with their coughs and sniffles and whatever other piffling ailments they can think of.'

'And what about those people who have hidden heart problems or kidney diseases?' she asked. 'I can be their first port of call. I might be the one who discovers what's wrong and starts them on the path to treatment. It's not just about sniffles and hypochondria.' She could feel her temper rising, and made an effort to calm down. Her father often had this effect on her, and she ought to know better than to rise to his bait.

Matt put his arm around her, squeezing her gently. 'Stick to your guns,' he mouthed.

'Are you going to talk to Sam or not?' her father pressed.

'Like I said, I don't think I can do that,' she said firmly.

'So you want me to come all the way over there when I'm up to my eyes in work? I have men working at full tilt, and we're still facing penalty clauses. I have to go and talk to site managers and electrical installers and you won't do one simple thing for me.'

She sucked in a deep breath. 'You can't shift the responsibility to me like that. How important is this partnership to you? If it's as significant as you're making it out to be, then it ought to be worth your while to come down here to see him and talk things through personally. It seems to me you've both been so caught up in work that you've lost the ability to communicate with one another.'

Matt's palm slid over her back, reassuringly warm and comforting, signalling his support.

Her father made an exasperated snort and cut the call.

'Oh, dear.' Lucy sighed. 'It's not good, is it? I mean, it sounds as though your father's decided to go ahead with quitting, but I always had the feeling he was in his element when he was working with my dad.'

'So did I.' Matt agreed. 'My mother's obviously been putting pressure on him, and while he's ill and vulnerable he doesn't have the energy to think things through properly.' His glance trailed over her in concern. 'Don't let it worry you. I think you did the right thing, standing up to your father. He strikes me as the sort of man who'll walk all over you if you show any sign of weakness. Perhaps that's where my father went wrong. He tries to fulfil people's expectations.'

'Maybe.' She was still smarting at her father's easy dismissal of her career. Of course he didn't mean it. He couldn't. After all, he'd been lucky so far, but he might well need a doctor's services one day. And wasn't his partner on the receiving end right now?

'I'll talk to my dad about it,' Matt promised, 'if it will put your mind at ease. He might want to delay making any moves until he's out of hospital and working under his own steam.'

'Thanks,' she said gratefully.

They went back to their patients, doing what they could to make them comfortable. Young William was ready to be discharged from hospital, and Lucy gave him a hug and wished him well. She was glad to see him looking so much stronger. 'You take care,' she said.

'Yeah, I will. See you.' Walking with a jaunty stride he left the ward with his mother a few minutes later, and Lucy went once more to see how Alice was doing.

After work that day, she went for a last fitting for her bridesmaid dress, and was thrilled with the result. What would Matt think when he saw her in it at the weekend? A small ripple of excitement ran through her. Perversely, despite all her worries about them being together, she wanted him to think she looked good.

On the day of the wedding she was filled with unexpected nerves mingled with the thrill of anticipation. She'd travelled to Amersham on the train with Matt that morning, and while he went off to find Ben at a local hotel to carry out his best-man duties, she'd gone to Jade's house to help the bride get ready. The wedding was scheduled for mid-afternoon, so they had ample time.

'You look beautiful,' she told Jade, when the preparations were complete and they were ready to set off for the church. Her friend's white dress clung in all the right places, emphasising her slender curves, while her hair was simply but perfectly styled, with a band of flowers for a headdress and finished off with an exquisite lace veil.

'The taxi's arrived,' Jade's mother said, and began to help Lucy shepherd the two small bridesmaids, Jade's cousins ages around six and seven years, and the page boy, age four, another cousin, into the waiting car.

'Don't they look adorable?' Mrs Blythe exclaimed. 'I love their dresses, with those wonderful overskirts and the pretty flowers in their hair. And as for you, Ryan,' she said, looking at her nephew, 'you look gorgeous in your trousers and waistcoat.' Ryan was shy, but Lucy saw that his cheeks dimpled as he clambered into the car.

A few minutes later, outside the church, Lucy gathered the youngsters together in readiness for the bride's appearance. 'Here she comes,' she whispered.

Music filled the church, with Wagner's triumphant wedding march playing as Jade walked down the aisle, her hand on her father's arm. Lucy smiled. They'd finally managed to get in touch with him after he'd sorted out a house move and he'd been overjoyed to come and 'give his daughter away.'

Ben turned to look at his bride, love and pride in his expression, and as the small procession moved level with the front set of pews, Lucy's

gaze tangled with Matt's. She saw the widening
of his eyes as she drew near, the look of wonder that sparked in their depths, but it was his
arrested expression that said it all, and a warm
glow came over her. He liked the way she looked.

She was wearing a dusky pink strapless dress
with a sweetheart neckline and ruched bodice,
and the skirt had a draped, gently flowing wrap-
over effect. It floated as she moved, brushing
against her ankles, and it made her feel ultra-
feminine.

Throughout the service, she was conscious of
Matt's intense blue gaze moving over her, and
afterwards, when the congregation assembled
in the churchyard, he came to stand with her as
she and her small charges threw confetti over the
happy couple.

'You take my breath away,' he said huskily. 'I
was trying to follow the service in the church,
but I couldn't take my eyes off you.'

'You don't look so bad yourself.' He looked terrific, in fact, with his dark, expensively tailored
suit emphasising the breadth of his shoulders,

and crisp, immaculate cuffs setting off the pale bronze of his skin. He wore a silk tie, and a stylish waistcoat, its deep red-wine colour matching the rose in his buttonhole.

'Well, thank you, ma'am,' he said with a flourish. 'Perhaps I could escort you to the ball?'

'I think that would be an excellent idea.' She looked down at the children in their bridal finery. 'How do you feel about our little entourage? I've a notion they're expecting all sorts of goodies when we get to the reception.'

He laughed. 'I'm pretty sure I can handle three little ones. Do you think they take bribes?'

She chuckled with him, and just at that moment they both looked up, into the flash of a camera lens. 'That was a beauty,' the cameraman said. 'Now let's have one of you both with the pageboy and younger bridesmaids.'

As soon as the wedding photos had been taken outside the church, they all went to the country house hotel where the reception was being held. They sat down to a wonderful wedding supper of prime rib beef, gratin potatoes, glazed pars-

nips and cracked peppercorn sauce, and just before dessert was served Matt stood up to make
his best man's speech.

He was good, Lucy thought, watching him de-
liver his speech. He did it with wit and charm,
causing everyone to break into laughter every
now and again. He toasted the bride and groom,
read out the cards, and then handed out gifts from
the bride and groom to the mothers of both parties, and to the pageboy and bridesmaids.

Lucy opened her gift when Matt sat down beside her once more and the guests were starting on their dessert. The black, silk-lined box
revealed an intricately designed gold bracelet
decorated with glistening gemstones. 'Oh, it's
lovely!' she exclaimed, turning to thank Jade and
Ben for the beautiful present.

'Let me help you with it,' Matt said, and she
held out her wrist to him, conscious of a pulse
beginning to flutter at the base of her throat when
his fingers brushed her arm and touched her skin
with fire.

He must have sensed her reaction, or perhaps

he felt it, too, because he held her hand for a fraction longer than was necessary and only let go when the young bridesmaids demanded that he help them, too. He gave Lucy a wry smile, but obliged them cheerfully enough.

Later in the evening, when the lights were dimmed and the disco started, they joined Jade and Ben with their guests on the dance floor, moving to the fast rhythm of the music, their bodies bathed in multicoloured darting lights that were projected from around the room. Perhaps she'd had a little too much wine, because the heavy beat echoed through her and filled her with exhilaration. Matt drew her close when the tempo slowed, lowering his head so that his cheek rested against her temple, and a thrill of sweet anticipation swirled through her from head to toe. She loved the feel of him, his hand at the base of her spine, the brush of his strong thighs against hers. She wanted more.

When the bride and groom left, about an hour later, they waved them off, and instead of going back into the reception room Matt took hold of

Lucy's hand and they walked together in the moonlight, following a path that wound its way through the hotel's landscaped gardens. He led her though a narrow archway and they came upon a secluded arbour, where white, star-shaped jasmine clambered over a rustic frame and filled the air with a heady, sweet scent.

He pulled her into his arms and her breath caught in her throat. Alone with him in this sheltered nook, she was conscious of the music throbbing in the distance, reverberating through her head, building to a crescendo of sound. She lifted her face to him and his mouth came down on hers, kissing her fiercely, feverishly, as though he couldn't help himself, couldn't wait any longer. He ran his hands over her soft curves, urging her closer, so that his thighs locked with hers and it seemed their bodies melded into one. His breathing was ragged. 'You're pure temptation,' he murmured against her throat, a groan starting up in the back of his throat as he moved against her. 'I tried to resist you…but I can't, I'm only human, Lucy…I need you.'

His heart was thumping so heavily that she could feel it against her breasts, a thunderous beat like a drum roll building to an explosive climax. She wanted him, desperately, needed to feel his body against hers, his lips trailing fire over her throat, the creamy slope of her shoulder, and lower, tracing the full, ripe curve of her breast. He let the tip of his tongue glide and dip beneath the bodice of her dress, and sensation ripped through her like the lick of flame.

The rush of blood roared in her ears, making her temples throb. His hand slid beneath her skirt, sliding over the velvet softness of her thigh, and heat shot through her. And then, out of the darkness, she heard the crunch of pebbles underfoot, scuffling sounds, followed by a moment of silence, and then the high-pitched sound of children's voices, coming closer.

'Lucy…where are you? Lucy?' a girl's voice called out in the semi darkness. 'My aunty sent me to find you. Where are you?'

Lucy swallowed hard, tried to stem the tide of desire that washed over her. 'I must answer her,' she whispered, the tips of her fingers moving shakily over Matt's chest.

Matt gave a shuddering, almost pained, groan. 'I know. I just…give me a minute.'

'Lucy?' Another voice called her name and there was a whispered conversation from the other side of the hedge. 'She must be out here. We've looked everywhere else.'

Lucy made a supreme effort and wrenched herself away from Matt, pulling air deep into her lungs, before saying in an even tone, 'It's all right. I'm here, girls.' She walked through the archway and looked down at her small nieces. 'Is it about the lift home?'

'Yes.' Both girls nodded. 'Aunty says if you and Matt can be ready in ten minutes, Jade's brother will drive you both back to London.'

'That's brilliant. Thanks, girls. Will you tell your aunty that we're coming now?'

'Okay.' The girls darted off along the path, without looking back.

Matt came through the archway to join her. 'I'd forgotten all about the lift home,' he said. He shot her a wry smile. 'Perhaps it's just as well the girls came along when they did. Things might have got a bit out of hand.'

'Yes.' She didn't know whether to be disappointed or relieved. Matt had been overcome with desire for her, and that was intensely exciting, thrilling her to the core, but ought she to tread more warily, think before she took that ultimate step of going to bed with him? She wasn't the kind of girl who took lovers indiscriminately. For her, sex had to be meaningful, based on love. And yet, so many times, she came across men who wanted her, told her they needed her, that she was the only woman they could ever desire. She'd learned to sift them out, the men who were just after one thing.

With Matt, the difference was he'd never acted that way, until now. Just a few moments ago they would have both thrown caution to the wind. But now she'd had time to cool down, she was able to think more clearly. She wanted him, longed to have him make love to her, and yet…he hadn't mentioned the one thing she needed to hear.

Love. It was the one word that would have made everything all right, but he hadn't said it. At the back of her mind there was an insistent thrumming, a warning bell that she tried to ignore. She could so easily be hurt if she gave everything to this relationship and then Matt decided to move on. She'd been hurt when Alex had betrayed her, but if the same thing happened with Matt, her life would fall apart.

'Are you all right?' Matt glanced at her as they walked back along the path towards the hotel. 'You're very quiet.'

'I'm okay. Perhaps I'm just a bit shocked by the interruption…it's left me feeling a bit shaky.'

He reached for her hand, tucking it into his palm. 'I got carried away. I never meant to come on so strong, but you look unbelievably beautiful. I'm burning up, aching for you.' He gave a short laugh. 'Lord knows what your father would think if he found out. He'd probably have a fit.'

She acknowledged that with a rueful smile. 'More than likely.'

They went back to the reception and met up

with Jade's brother James and his fiancée. 'It was a great day for them, wasn't it?' James said, looking back at the wedding debris, scattered petals of confetti, balloons and party poppers. 'They looked really happy.'

Lucy smiled. 'They did.'

They said their goodbyes and set off for home. It was well after midnight by now, and the street was dark and quiet when James dropped them off outside the London house. Sitting next to Matt in the intimacy of the back of the car, both of them hidden in the shadows, she'd been in a constant state of hyper-awareness. He held her hand in his, his long legs nudging hers, and for all her doubts and uncertainties she wanted the journey to end so that she could be alone with him once more. She was overcome by a heightened sense of expectancy.

They waved off James and his fiancée and went into the house, shutting the front door behind them. The glow from the security light threw soft shadows across the hallway, and in the darkness they brushed against one another. She heard

Matt's sharp intake of breath and she reached for him, running her hand along his arm. She knew it was adding the spark to his tinder, but she couldn't help herself, and when Matt gently urged her against the wall, leaning over her and kissing her soundly, she was glad. She wound her arms around his neck and pressed her body to his, throwing caution to the wind. His breathing was coming in soft, short bursts, as though he was struggling to get air into his lungs.

'You know exactly what that does to me, don't you?' He trailed kisses over her cheek, her throat, and gave a shuddery sigh. 'Ah, Lucy, you drive me crazy with wanting you…but…' He gently eased himself away from her, holding her lightly, at arm's length. 'Here,' he whispered, 'in this place…it feels wrong.'

All at once, without warning, the hall light snapped on, and they broke apart in startled surprise. Lucy's father stood in the hallway, glowering at both of them.

'So this is how you keep your word, huh?' he shot at Matt, grinding the words between his teeth. 'You're quite happy to take advantage of my daughter under my own roof?'

'That's not how it is,' Matt answered, his tone clipped. 'I'm not taking advantage of her.'

'It's how I see it. It's not enough that your father let me down, is it? It must be a family trait.'

'What are you doing here, Dad?' Lucy interrupted, bracing herself.

'I'm staying the night. I had to come over here to see Sam as you wouldn't help out.' He continued to glower at her. 'I can see why that was now. You're too busy cavorting with the tenants.'

'Tenants…in the plural?' Lucy said, her mouth curling around the word with contempt. 'Did you mean to be so insulting? No, don't answer that. I can see you're in no mood for a logical discussion.' She glared at him. 'As to Matt and I…I'm old enough to decide for myself how I live my life. It's time you understood that. And if I choose to be with Matt, I don't see that it's any business of yours.'

'I'm still your father, and you owe me some respect, don't forget that. In fact, you owe me a whole lot more, but you seem to take it all for granted.' His dark eyes glittered with anger. 'We'll talk about this in the morning. I'm going to bed.'

He marched up the stairs, leaving Matt and Lucy to face each other in the hallway.

'I'm sorry about that,' she said. 'He'll get over it. It must have been a shock to him to find us, that's all.'

'You always defend him, but there are times when he goes too far.' Matt's jaw set in a hard line, and his eyes were dark with anger. 'He talks about my father as though Dad owes him something, when in reality he's probably pushed him way beyond what was reasonable.'

She couldn't let him get away with that. 'I don't believe it's just that he pushed him. Your father was perfectly capable of setting limits on what he would, or wouldn't, do and he obviously chose not to do that.'

Matt's mouth made a flat line. 'I still don't think he was able to stand up to the pressure. I've seen how your father treats you, and it's wrong.

He can't go on doing this, dictating how people live their lives. And if he's intent on causing trouble at the hospital, I'll have to stop him. I'll not have him upset my father.'

'He won't do that, I'm sure of it.' His anger was fuelling her own, and she spoke firmly, emphasising each point. 'He's not perfect, he's never been perfect, but he talks without thinking. He'll come round by morning and see that he's not being fair. My father's not a bad man. He makes mistakes. We all make mistakes sometimes.'

'Perhaps he makes more than most,' Matt said flatly.

'That's unfair.' She frowned, wishing they could lay this to rest, wishing her father had never turned up. 'Matt, you're not even trying to understand him. He says what's on his mind, but that's not necessarily a bad thing. He's always been blunt and to the point, but he can be reasonable, too.'

He shook his head. 'Perhaps he's the one who needs to understand. You, too. You're always making excuses for him. Well, I can't do this any more, Lucy. I won't do it. I'm not going to be one of his tenants any longer. I'm moving out.'

She stared at him, shocked to the core. 'But where will you go? You don't have to do this, surely? I don't want you to go, Matt.'

'I'm sorry, but that's how it is. I'm not staying. It's over. I'll get my things together and leave in the morning.' Grim faced, he turned away from her. He went to the kitchen and rummaged in one of the cupboards, coming back with a hold-all. She realised he meant to start packing that very night, and she suddenly felt as though she couldn't breathe. Her stomach felt like lead. How would she go on without him?

CHAPTER NINE

'IT'S over.' Those words echoed through Lucy's mind again and again over the next couple of days. She'd been hurt beyond belief when Matt had moved out the next morning, with hardly a word spoken between them. It made her feel ill to see him go.

And even though she saw him at work the following day, he was preoccupied, busy making phone calls to various people, and she guessed he was sorting out a place to stay.

It was strange to wander through the rooms of the empty house now that he had gone. She was desolate without him. She didn't want to eat. She couldn't sleep. It was a miserable way to go on, but she didn't know what she could do to put things right.

'Is you going off to work soon?' Jacob peered

over the top of the fence as she broke up pieces of stale scones and spread them out on the bird table.

'Yes, in a few minutes,' she answered. She glanced at him. He looked as unhappy as she felt, and from the tear streaks running down his cheeks, she guessed he had been crying. 'What's wrong, Jacob?' she asked, going over to him. 'Has something upset you?'

He nodded. 'We can't find Henry,' he said, his voice breaking up. 'He's lost.'

'Henry?' she repeated, at a loss. 'Oh, do you mean your cat?'

He nodded. 'He didn't come in this morning for his breakfast. He always comes when I rattle the box of biscuits, but today he didn't.' Tears ran down his cheeks, and Lucy wanted to hug him tight and console him.

'Perhaps he's just gone on a little adventure,' she said. 'I'm sure he'll turn up. He's not been missing for too long, after all.' She had a quick look around the garden, but there was no sign of the white cat. 'If he doesn't turn up soon, your mum and dad can perhaps put up some posters in the neighbourhood. I'm sure someone will find him and bring him home to you.'

He perked up a bit at that, but Lucy was sombre as she made her way to work. The boy's distress had been genuine, and it seemed to be on a par with her own. If only she could put up posters and have Matt returned to her…

She'd reached the hospital's main entrance when her phone rang. Her father's name came up on the display and she winced. They hadn't spoken since he'd gone to see Matt's father, and she had no idea of the outcome of that visit because he'd gone straight back to Berkshire afterwards. She hadn't had it in her to phone him.

'How are you?' she asked. 'Did you manage to sort out your problems with Sam?'

'We're working on it,' he said briefly. 'I heard that Matt is moving out. His father told me. Is it true?'

'Yes. He's already gone.'

'I see.'

He fell silent, and Lucy said in a sombre tone, 'Why would he stay, in the circumstances?'

'Why wouldn't he? I didn't expect him to leave. He's the son of my oldest friend.'

She didn't answer him and he said gruffly, 'I said some things I shouldn't—to you—the other night. It was late, I was worried about this partnership thing—you know I don't mean those things, don't you?'

'I know.'

She walked to the lift bay, and her father said, 'You'd better advertise for more students to take over the accommodation. Jade and Ben won't be coming back, of course. As to Matt, he might reconsider, if you put it to him.'

'No, he won't.' She stepped into the lift as the doors opened. 'I have to go to work now, Dad. Was there anything else you wanted?'

'No. No, that was all.'

'Okay. Bye. Give my love to Mum.'

'I will.'

She found Matt on the children's ward, looking through the files at the nurses' station.

'Hi,' he said. 'Will it be all right with you if I come back to the house later on this evening to fetch some of the things I left behind?'

'Yes, of course.'

'I didn't have room to take them with me when I moved out. There's a spare amplifier, some medical books and a lamp, and so on. Bits and pieces.'

'Yes, that's fine.' She didn't know how to talk to him. It felt wrong, as though they were strangers, not two people who had shared passionate, exhilarating kisses just a couple of days ago. How could things have gone so wrong between them? She said slowly, 'Where are you living now? You managed to find a place quickly enough.'

'I'm looking after a friend's flat while he's away on holiday for the next fortnight. It'll be long enough for me to sort things out.'

'Yes, I suppose it will.' She frowned. 'How is your father? I hope my dad's visit didn't set him back in any way?'

'No, it didn't. He's feeling much better, actually. Mr Sheldon did the angioplasty yesterday, and everything went really well. He'll be on medication now, to keep his blood pressure down and make sure his blood doesn't clot easily, and generally they'll keep an eye on him in Outpatients from now on.'

'Your mother must be pleased about that.'

'Yes, she is. She's much more relaxed. Of course, she'll be watching his diet like a hawk, to make sure he keeps off the fatty foods and doesn't overdo the drink.' He smiled. 'He's happy with the way things are going, and he seems to have learned a lesson about doing too much work. He's promised her that he'll learn to delegate and keep work things from nine to five now, five days a week. Kyle's going to step in as a manager—my father hadn't wanted to let go of the reins until now, but I think that will probably work out well.'

'I'm glad for you.'

He gave her a quizzical look. 'How are you? Have you patched things up with your father?'

She nodded. 'He's already phoned and apologised to me. I knew he didn't mean what he said. You perhaps overreacted, walking out like that.'

His eyes darkened. 'It was for the best, Lucy. I've thought for a while that I should be looking for a place of my own.'

'So you'd have gone anyway?' she asked disconsolately.

'Yes, eventually.'

Mandy came over to the desk just then and handed him a file. 'It's the endocrinologist's report on Alice,' she said, 'the toddler with the parathyroid problem.'

'Ah, yes. She had the operation yesterday, didn't she?'

'She did,' Mandy said. 'And I thought you might like to know—I went over to Neonatal, and they have the CT scan results on baby Sarah. She's fine. It doesn't look as though there's going to be any brain damage…nothing lasting, anyway.'

'That's brilliant, Mandy. Thanks for checking.' He smiled at Lucy, who breathed a sigh of relief, and then he glanced through the report on Alice.

He handed it to her. 'Apparently the tumour was benign. The surgeon took it out—no problems, and she seems to be doing well. We'll need to keep an eye on her medication over the next week or two, but once things settle down, she should be fine.'

'Oh, that's brilliant news. Her parents will be so relieved.' Lucy read through the consultant's report, glad that things had turned out so well for the little girl.

She spent the rest of the morning helping Matt with the children on the ward, and she was pleased that all of them seemed to be doing all right. There were a couple of new admissions, and Matt went to examine them and write up their notes, while she went to see how Tom was getting on.

His level of sedation had gradually been re-duced, and yesterday, once he had opened his eyes, Matt had removed his endotracheal tube. He had been sleepy, though, and they'd had no real chance to assess whether he had suffered any brain damage.

Over the course of the morning Lucy had no-ticed more restless movements in his limbs, and for her that was good news, but the boy's parents didn't seem to have noticed. Tom's grandmother sat with them, and the atmosphere between the three of them was tense.

'The coffee in those machines is too bitter,' Tom's father was saying. 'I didn't choose black, but that's more or less what came out.'

'Why don't you try the cafeteria?' Mrs Cavendish suggested. 'I don't think it's too bad in there.'

'Why do you think?' he snapped. 'I don't want to have to leave my boy's bedside.'

'It was only a suggestion,' his mother-in-law said, her voice rising.

'Why are you shouting at each other?' It was barely above a whisper, but all three of them turned in sudden shock to see that the child was watching them, his eyes open, blinking at the hospital lights.

'Oh, sweetheart…you're awake!' His mother was overjoyed, reaching for his hand and holding it between hers.

His father could barely speak for a moment or

two because he was so choked up. Then he said, 'Well done, lad. You're back with us.'

'You were cross with Gran,' the boy said.

'Oh, that was nothing. We were just upset, that's all. We've been so worried about you. Your gran and I will get on fine, won't we?' He turned to look at his wife's mother, and she nodded.

'Of course we will. I'm so glad you're all right, Tom.' She glanced at Jack. 'I'm sorry if I've been hard on you these last few days. It was the shock, I think.'

'It's okay. Forget it. It doesn't matter now.'

Lucy quietly went about her work, checking the monitors, making sure that Tom was comfortable. It seemed that he would be all right. And perhaps his family would be okay, too.

She went home with Matt at the end of the day, and it was almost like old times. He was still the same with her, joking, teasing, as though nothing had happened. She didn't understand it. How could he be the same when she was breaking up inside?

She made coffee for them both, and Matt made one of his pizzas, and they sat and ate together and everything was so normal she wanted to cry for all that she'd lost. Instead, she steeled herself to act as though nothing at all was amiss.

Afterwards, she went with him out into the garden, so that he could rummage about in the shed for the bits and pieces he wanted to take to his new place.

'Have you any idea where you'll live when your friend comes back from his holiday?' she asked. 'I suppose there are plenty of flats to rent in the city. They might be a bit pricey, though.'

'I won't be renting,' he said. 'I'm looking to buy a house.'

'Oh, I see,' she said in surprise. 'Still, I suppose you might as well. Better to put money into property than waste it on rent.' She frowned. 'Do you have somewhere in mind?'

He nodded. 'I wanted to talk to you about that.' They stopped by the old apple tree, heavy with slowly ripening fruit. 'I've been looking at the waterfront house. I know how much you want it, and I thought maybe we could put in an offer.'

Her mouth dropped open. 'We?' She stared at him. 'What are you suggesting? That we live together?'

'Now, there's a thought.' He grinned. 'I can just imagine your father's reaction to that. No, of course not.'

'Then I don't understand. Saturday night you told me it was over between us. I was devastated, and now…' Her voice broke on the words. 'And now you're suggesting we buy a house together— a house I can't even afford?'

He frowned, looking at her oddly. 'Over between us? I didn't say anything of the sort. Where did you get that idea from?'

'"I'm not staying. It's over. I'll get my things together…" That's what you said.' She'd been so upset she remembered his exact words and now she threw them back at him.

'I meant, it's over, me living in this house— your father's house.' He put his arms around her, holding her close. 'How could it possibly be over between us when I care about you so much?'

'But...' Relief washed over her. He hadn't meant what she'd thought. She gazed at him in bewilderment. 'You do?'

'Of course. Surely you know that?'

'Well, I...' Her brows drew together. 'The other day...in the hallway, after the wedding, you didn't seem to want me. And then you said you were leaving. I didn't know what to think.'

'Ah, Lucy, you don't know how hard it's been for me. I've wanted you so badly it hurt. Being with you here, day after day, wanting you and not being able to do anything about it—you can't imagine how difficult it was for me.'

'I didn't know. You never said...'

'How could I?' He gave a wry smile. 'I know how you feel about men constantly making a play for you. I didn't want to be like all the others. I want you for who you are, not just for the way you look.' He hesitated. 'Besides, it wouldn't have been right to take advantage of you while I was a tenant in your house, would it? It would have felt all wrong.' He smiled wryly again. 'And if he'd had his way, your father would have booted me from here to Timbuktu if I'd so much as breathed too close to you.'

'Surely not?' She was stunned by the revelation. He'd never said a word, given her no inkling of the intensity of what he'd been feeling. And as for her father's involvement… 'He wouldn't do that—you're like part of the family, his partner's son.'

He gave a short laugh. 'Don't you believe it. You said yourself he vets everyone who has anything whatever to do with you. And that means everyone. He did it to me.'

She pulled in a shaky breath. 'I can hardly believe what you're saying. Did he really warn you off? When?'

He nodded. 'Way back, when I first moved into the house. I understood that he had your welfare at heart, but he needn't have worried. I would never have taken advantage of our situation. It would have felt wrong somehow.'

She was still shocked by his revelation, but

after a moment she said sorrowfully, 'I thought he would let go when I was twenty one, but now, three years later, it's beginning to look as though it's never going to happen.'

'Oh, I don't know about that. I think the process has already started. After all, you stood up to him, didn't you? That's why he came over on the day of the wedding, because you finally stood your ground. And you did the same again that night in the hallway. Perhaps that was what I was waiting for—for you to be ready to break away and finally make decisions for yourself. I hoped you'd decide that you wanted me. Anyway, it made me realise I had to leave and prepare the way for both of us to be together.'

She glanced at him fleetingly, her silky lashes veiling her eyes. 'I'd no idea you felt that way about me…that you were holding back.'

'I didn't want to do anything to upset the apple cart. But it was hard. I cared so much for you. I wanted to show you how I felt, I wanted to put my arms around you, hold you—and those mornings, when you were half-asleep, wandering along the corridor with your hair all tousled and your robe slipping down off your shoulders…'

His voice became rough around the edges, his gaze wandering over her, while Lucy simply stared at him, wide-eyed, as he added, 'More and more, I'd find myself fighting the urge to slide it off you completely.'

Startled, her eyes widened and her lips parted a fraction. 'You did?' The words came out on a silent breath of air, and warm colour filled her cheeks. 'So…so why leave it until now to tell me?' She couldn't get to grips with what was happening. Things had changed so much in these last few weeks. The man she'd known had always been there, part of the gang, a fixture in her everyday life, and yet it seemed as though she hadn't really known him at all. These last few weeks had been a huge learning curve. She was finding out more and more about him as every day passed.

He sighed. 'Now, that's a difficult one.' His mouth made a flat line, briefly. 'I think, deep down, I didn't want to frighten you off. I knew how you felt about men in general and, as long as I was kind of invisible around you, I guessed it probably wouldn't matter. Then there were the exams coming up. You had so much on your mind, and I knew how important they were to you. I didn't want to do anything to ruin that for you.'

'And now?'

'Now it's getting too hard for me to handle. Working with you throughout the day, being at home alone with you when Jade and Ben were away, it's brought us closer together, and all the time temptation's just an arm's length away.' His eyes darkened as he moved closer to her. 'I've realised I'm not made of stone. I want you… I want to hold you and kiss you, and show you how much I care for you.'

She gazed up at him, her blue eyes glimmering with invitation. He cared for her, wanted her… wasn't that how she felt about him? 'Then why not give in to temptation?'

He exhaled raggedly, his body jerking as though she'd just touched him with a live wire. Then he shook himself down and said softly, 'You're a temptress, a seductive, alluring woman, and I'm just a helpless man. I've been on a slow burn for months, and now, when you look at me that way, I feel I'm sliding into a meltdown. How am I supposed to find the strength to resist you?'

He ran his hand lightly down her arm and leaned towards her, bending his head so that his forehead gently rested against hers for a second or two.

Her mind was in a whirl. He wanted her, and it wasn't just a passing fancy, it had been building up for a long while. She put her arms around him and held him close. 'I want you, too,' she whispered.

He kissed her then, a fierce, achingly sweet kiss that made her feel as though she was burning up with fever. Her soft curves were crushed against his strong body, and she drank him in, wanting everything he had to offer. A soft sigh escaped her lips and she looked into his eyes, 'I love you,' she murmured.

'Ah…you don't know how good that makes me

feel.' He kissed her again, his hands moving over her, caressing, stroking along the length of her spine. Then he said in a soft, questioning tone, 'So…maybe I was right in thinking about buying the house?'

'I'm not sure I understand about that.'

He tilted her chin with his fingers. 'I meant it to be for us. I love you, Lucy. I don't even know when I first realised it. It sort of grew on me. I think that's when I first started thinking I ought to move out. And then we saw the waterfront house, and I knew you wanted it more than anything. So I told your father I wanted to buy it.'

She was stunned. 'But how? What did he say to that? You and he haven't exactly been getting on like a house on fire just lately, have you?'

He smiled, gently tucking a golden strand of her hair back behind her ear when it fell across her cheek. 'Well, you could call it a kind of deal-breaker, I suppose. My father suggested he would consider staying in the partnership if I had first option on the house—at a reasonable price, of course.'

'And my father agreed to that?'

'Strangely enough, he did.'

She let out a long, slow breath, trying to think this through. 'But your mother would never be happy about that, would she? She doesn't want your father back in partnership, and she certainly wouldn't want to do business with my father.' A sudden thought struck her. 'Does she know about you and me?'

She looked up at him, and he dropped a kiss onto her forehead. 'Yes.' He smiled. 'She's actually softened up quite a bit since my dad had his operation. She was wound up very tightly, you know, and I think she was looking for someone to blame. I've talked to her about it, and she realises things got out of hand.'

'So she doesn't mind about you and me?'

'She doesn't mind. I think she'll actually be quite pleased when she has more time to think about it. I know my dad is happy about you and I getting together.'

'Mmm… About that, what exactly did you have in mind?'

'Marriage?' It was a question as much as a statement, and he must have realised that he was doing things all the wrong way around because he said gently, 'Will you marry me, Lucy? Please say yes, because I have the future all planned out, and I need you to go along with it because you're an integral part of it.'

She laughed. 'So that's what I'm to tell our children, is it? I had to marry you because your plan wouldn't work without me?'

'Well, sort of, yes. I hadn't thought much beyond buying the house and then getting married. I can't imagine the future, my future, without you.' He frowned. 'Did you just mention our children?'

She wrapped her arms around his neck. 'I did. And of course they'll need a wonderful house where they can grow up happy…with a few safety measures built in around the waterfront, of course. How on earth can we afford it?'

'That's all right. I've made quite a lot of money over the years, selling my songs and music and playing gigs here and there. I've invested most of it, with my father's advice—he's pretty shrewd at these sorts of things—and I've made enough for us to be comfortable. So it's not a problem. All I need is for you to say that you'll marry me, and the rest will follow.'

'Yes,' she said, reaching up to kiss him tenderly. 'Oh, yes, please.'

He bent his head to hers and he kissed her, wrapping his arms even more firmly about her. But in the silence of those few minutes, when they were locked in each other's embrace, they heard a strange mewling sound.

Slowly, they broke off the kiss and looked around. 'It's coming from the shed,' she murmured. 'It sounds like Jacob's cat, Henry. He said he'd lost him.'

'If it is him, perhaps he got in through the open windows—or maybe it was when you put the watering cans away. You do that every evening, don't you, after you've watered the plants?'

'Oh, heavens, what have I done?' Lucy was aghast at the thought she might have unwittingly locked up the poor cat.

Matt opened the shed door and peered inside. 'Well, well,' he said. 'You just have to come and see this.'

'What is it?' She followed him to the door.

'I think Henry must be a Henrietta...otherwise something very strange is going on. Are those five kittens I see? Or is it six?'

'Oh, let me see.' She looked inside the shed, and there were six kittens, snuggled up inside an old basket, with Henry-etta. She was licking each of them in turn. 'Oh, they're so sweet, aren't they?' she exclaimed. 'I can't wait to tell Jacob. He'll be so thrilled.'

'Mmm... Can we put a hold on that for a minute or two? I think we were in the middle of sealing a very special bargain.'

She laughed, gazing up at him. They propped open the shed door with their bodies as they held one another close and kissed once more. Lucy was in a state of sheer bliss, loving the way he dropped soft kisses on her cheek, her throat and then traced his way back to her mouth once more.

'I love you,' she murmured.

'Mmm…me, too. I'll love you forever and a day.' He kissed her again and for the next few minutes there was quiet throughout the garden, except for the gentle sound of birdsong.

And then… 'What you doing?' a small voice piped up from the side of the garden, and they both began to laugh.

* * * * *